THE DAVID CHRONICLES
Volume III

The Edge of Revolt

USA Today
Bestselling Author

UVI POZNANSKY

The Edge of Revolt©2014 Uvi Poznansky

This novel can be read as a standalone novel, as well as a part of The David Chronicles, a trilogy in the voice of David, describing his youth, prime of life, and old age: Rise to Power A Peek at Bathsheba The Edge of Revolt

Published by Uviart
P.O. Box 3233 Santa Monica CA 90408
Blog: uviart.blogspot.com
Email: uvi.author@gmail.com

First Edition
Printed in the United States of America
Book design, cover image and design by
Uvi Poznansky

Contents

Prologue

In recent years, I have been granted rest from all my enemies around the land, but peace has brought no calm to my heart, because God knows how many plots are being hatched, at this moment, by enemies from within.

The time when I was considered a menace to the throne is long gone, alerting me to one idea that holds true to this day: the crown is always in danger of being snatched away. So in my present position I should not tolerate any hint of revolt.

At my age I should expect nothing but respect. But when my own son walks away from me, my resolve immediately falters. To spite me, he smiles flirtatiously at Abishag, my lovely new concubine, till she tightens her robe around her waist and turns her head away, hiding her blush from him, and perhaps from me, too. Then with a youthful vigor, Adoniah bangs the heavy iron door deliberately behind him, which makes Goliath's sword clang against the wall, right here over my head.

The rattle shocks me into trying to overcome the fright, the sudden quaking of my bones.

I adore my son, which lures me into seeing myself—my own image, only more invincible—in him. So what if he is rebellious? I must have been the same way at his age. Back then, did I not leave my father, exchanging the safety of his home for something unknown, for adventure? Did I not defy his charge for me to remain there, in Hebron, and support him in his time of need?

Never before have I considered how the old man must have felt, left behind in fragile health, in a crumbling house, with not one of us children staying there to keep him company—no one but loneliness.

Her face still rosy with a sense of embarrassment, Abishag wipes the little smile from her lips and curtseys before me. She is obedient, perhaps even fearful of me. Plumping herself on my blankets, she goes back to holding the inkwell for me.

I dip the tip of my feather in it, glancing at the veins marbling my thinning, nearly transparent skin. Is this my hand? Why is it trembling so? It seems to be my father's, and so does my voice, when I utter the words as I scribble them, *"When I kept silent, my bones wasted away, through my groaning all day long. For day and night, your hand was heavy on me. My strength was sapped, as in the heat of summer."*

My father is gone. Finding myself now in his place is a humbling surprise. I know I deserve it.

So I ask myself, how can I blame my son? His mother keeps telling me that he is restless, which must be my fault, of course, for not giving him a role or any kind of training in governing the land. It is too early for that. I mean, why should I loosen my hold on power? I am still the king, am I not? So I keep telling her that I am training him in patience. Adoniah is still young. His life is ahead of him. He can wait a little while longer.

Seeing how exhausted I am Abishag takes the feather, ever so gently, from my fingers, careful not to touch the tip, and withdraws from me. Washing the ink off at the other end of the chamber, she bends over the windowsill, glancing at the lush trees swaying down there, in the royal gardens. Without words, she hums a little tune under her breath, and her voice is so sad, so melodious, that it tells me how desperately she misses her faraway village, from where she was taken to the palace.

She must have been eager, at first, to meet the notoriously dashing young hero, the slayer of Goliath, the idol drawn so perfectly out of legends that belong to a dying generation. Only now does she realize that I belong nowhere else but in her aging mother's dreams.

I tell her, "Listen, daughter, and pay careful attention. Forget your people and your father's house. Let the king be enthralled by your beauty. Honor him, for he is your lord."

And at once I wonder, why do I take this fatherly tone with her, all of a sudden? And why do I speak of myself as if I were not here?

Abishag cannot help but yawn, which I happen to understand, because the lecture I have aimed at her bores me, too.

"So many young men, out there," she whispers.

"So much noise," I complain, over her excitement.

"If it's disturbing to you, your majesty, I can go down," she offers. "I can ask them to keep things more quiet, for you."

"No," say I. "Stay with me."

"Are you cold? Shall I close the curtains?"

"No. Keep them open."

Then, with slight hesitation, "Your son," she says. "What does he want? Why did he come?"

7

"He loves me so," I say, hoping she would not catch the irony in my voice. "Once in a long while he comes up here, to check if I'm still breathing."

Abishag says nothing in reply. After a long pause she asks, "Did he invite you to the festivities? I would love to escort you —"

"Festivities?" say I. "No one tells me anything these days, which is why I am becoming so pitifully suspicious."

"I see him down there," she says. "His guests are arriving now, gathering around to greet him. They're laughing. He's not."

At that I wave my hand. "Adoniah must be tired. He's utterly weary of life here, in my palace. Luxury can be such a boring thing when you're born into it."

She glances back at me, her eyes wide with disbelief. "Is it, really?"

"It must be," say I. "Unlike me, he's never fought for what he has. To entertain him, his mother throws one party after another in his honor."

"He's young," says Abishag. "And so tense. She just wants to make him happy."

"As you may know, her name, Haggith, stands for celebration, which suited her perfectly well several decades ago, when I first cuddled her in my arms. How eloquently I praised her beauty, back then! Alas, how quickly it has waned! Gone is my delight —"

"That," says Abishag, in her dreamy voice, "is the nature of it, is it not?"

"Perhaps so," I say. "But now, in heaven's name, what is there to celebrate? That, I'm afraid, is yet unclear to me."

"Does a party need a reason? Sometimes," she says, "it's just for fun."

"Fun? Not at this extravagant cost," I counter. "My wife thinks I don't know the extent of her expenses. Lately she's stopped asking me to authorize them. Instead, she simply acts as if my entire treasure already belongs to her son, simply because."

"Because what?"

"Because he's entitled. According to her, giving no reason at all for this squandering is much more convincing than the best excuse."

I prop myself up on my pillows to catch sight of Haggith. There she is, wearing her best winter gown, which is puffy here, tight there, and fleecy all around, elaborately designed to give her flesh a much needed lift in all the right places.

With great jubilation, my wife is chatting about nothing worth mentioning, first with one guest, then another, all the while lavishing rich food upon them. The rest of my wives—Michal, Ahinoam, Abigail, Maachah, Abital, Eglah, and Bathsheba—stay away from her, perhaps in the women's quarters. She pays no attention to them. After all, her son is next in the line of succession. He is the heir-apparent, now that his elder brothers—my firstborn Amnon and my beloved Absalom—have perished.

Now Abishag unties her robe. She wears some lacy nothing underneath, which reveals more of her flesh than it manages to conceal. With a rhythmic step, she comes back to bed and clings dutifully to me, her heat surrounding my coolness.

Caressing me, "David," she whispers.

"Hush, now," I mutter. "I'm tired. Don't want to talk anymore."

Mine is a strange grief. Bringing the boys back to mind paralyzes me in a way that words cannot describe. Let me stop torturing myself, stop unearthing the past, trying to find out what I could have done differently to change what happened between them, between us.

Is the search futile? How far back should I go? What purpose is served by recalling this mistake or the other? What is the value of remorse? Can it bring back the dead?

Stop thinking. Stop being me. Let me bury the memories, all of them. But how can I, when Adoniah is now as tall as Amnon used to be, and he has started to grow his hair long, which conjures a sudden apparition in my mind, a vision of my Absalom, hanging—

I blink away the tears. Adoniah thinks that already I am becoming soft, like a babe. Believe me, I wish he were right. For me, a feeble mind would be such bliss.

I turn away from Abishag, knowing she would be cupping her ears if she hears me sigh one more time. And to the wall, I plead, *"How long, Lord? Will you forget me forever? How long will you hide your face from me? How long must I wrestle with my thoughts, and day after day have sorrow in my heart?"*

No longer do I hope for redemption. All I have left—when prayers go unanswered—is simple pleasures. Let me feel the touch, the soothing touch of evening breeze. It passes through, lifting the edge of the curtain, bringing in faint, distant sounds of wine splashing, glasses clinking. Laughter.

In flat, monotonous tones, which are so different from my own, Adoniah gives a toast to himself. I lean in his direction and cup my ears to listen. He promises his guests that tomorrow the party will come to its height with a new announcement. Until then, the whole thing must be kept secret. I imagine he is smiling victoriously, and raising his goblet, which used to be mine. All that stands in his way is a fragile, elderly man.

I block his voice and the cheers of his mother and all his guests, who are clapping at the end of each sentence, by mumbling under my breath, *"You prepare a table before me in the presence of my enemies. You anoint my head with oil. My cup overflows"*—but somehow, the words fail to convince me of my good fortune.

I am curious how splendidly they will celebrate my death.

Pressing the pillow tightly over my head I try not to hear them—all of these strangers, and my son, a stranger too—drowning idle talk with one drink after another, and loitering along the table with bouts of silly laughter.

For a while, sleep must have overtaken me. With a sudden start I raise myself on my elbows. I listen. The party is over. My eyes are heavy, but I force them open. Abishag slumbers fitfully, her arms bound around my neck, her face turned away, flushed with desire, her mouth yearning to be kissed—but not by me.

I used to be so skilled with women. Now my decrepit body lays bare before her. There is no need to cover myself, because my chill comes from within. I shiver, knowing I cannot take her. She is—and will forever remain—a maiden.

As I slip away from her touch, the sleeping girl waves her hand in the air like one flicking off an annoying fly. Then she curls like a baby over her knees.

Supported by my scepter I begin lumbering barefoot across the chamber. Its darkness is dabbed here and there with a silvery ray of moonshine, which allows me to find my way, somehow, around the furniture to the other side, to the windowsill.

Torches are flickering out there, along the path leading to the royal gardens. On the other side of the flames Adoniah sits alone at the head of the table. Half a smile is twitching on his face, contorting it, so it is hard for me to distinguish satisfaction from bitterness. I ask myself what is the best thing I can do for him.

By his expression I read the answer. Expire.

No, that cannot be true. My heart goes out to him. What a sensitive, sweet child he used to be. Why does he hate me so? How did it come to that?

Now Adoniah lifts his hand, and plows across puddles and spills of red wine, while staring blankly at the waste. Leftover pastries are strewn among the stains, all over the richly embroidered tablecloth. Remnants of flowery decorations are dangling here and there, in disarray, from the moonlit branches.

He licks his sticky finger, flicks off some stale crumbs, and peers at his empty glass.

I think I spot a spark, a mad flash in his eye. What does he see there? Why does he shake his head and start talking to himself, as if to rehearse a speech? I suppose that for him, silence is something he cannot easily ignore.

I should talk to my son, help him overcome his anger. We should try to mend things between us. But before I can call out to him Adoniah raises his head, casting a look directly at my chamber window. The flame between us outlines only one side of his face. Ferocious intensity seems to be burning in his eye. Perhaps it is nothing but a reflection of torchlight.

I am quite certain that blinded by the light, he cannot spot me—yet without even thinking I raise my scepter, as if to defend myself, and sink back into the darkest dark.

"Beware," I whisper.

Whatever else I may have lost during the years of my decline, the instinct of a fighter is still in me, which I find amazing. I hope it will go on sustaining me to the very end.

*

It is then—as I retreat from watching him—that I sense a presence directly behind me. Stumbling into her I utter a cry. She must be as startled as I am, as I find myself wrapped in her arms.

"You!" I gasp. "What are you doing here, at this time of night?"

She says nothing, but presses a finger to my lips. Glancing over her shoulder at the sleeping girl, Bathsheba takes my hand without uttering a single word.

There is no sound except the creaking of hinges as we open the twin doors and step outside, onto the roof. Since the beginning of our affair this has always been our place, away from all the others. But in recent years we have neglected to come here, because the place has changed, as if to suggest clues of a crime.

The lovely wooden lattice that used to stand there, marking the edge of the roof, has remained broken since that horrific event, I mean, the rape of every woman in my harem, a few winters back. The slats are still hanging loose, swaying in the wind in wait of repair, and the vine that used to thread itself over and under them has withered away. Gone are all its blossoms. Even its thorns have shriveled to dust, so the view is open and completely unobstructed. And so are we, standing there, feeling exposed before the windows, the holes in the distance, the frozen eyes of the city.

Tonight, the landscape seems lifeless. There is no motion anywhere, except for the clouds. They are rolling in, hanging full and dark over the hills of Jerusalem, roaming over us like an upside down flock of sheep.

"D'you have to ask?" says Bathsheba, as if to tease me. Her voice is measured, but knowing her I detect the note of urgency in it. "You know exactly why I'm here."

To which I say, "I do," even though the truth is different. I do not want to know.

"Do you," she counters. "Have you read the scroll? The one I've left with you?"

And before I have a chance to say that I will, and ask for grace and patience, she goes on to demand, "What will you do, then, about what's written there?"

I have no need for the scroll. In spite of what she thinks of my lack of attention I can guess, quite accurately, the latest rumors. The game—the fierce competition for the throne, which claimed the lives of my elder sons, Amnon and Absalom—is now threatening to repeat itself, playing out between Adoniah and my younger child, Solomon.

"Beware," says Bathsheba. "If you wait till tomorrow it'll be too late."

By the tremble in her voice she knows, and so does everyone in the palace, how vulnerable I am, in my condition. Come morning I may be toppled from the throne.

The festivities in the royal gardens will culminate in a hasty move, a coronation, which will be announced in the time-honored tradition of all riots: without bothering to ask for the blessing of the current monarch. And then, then there will be a bloodbath. I sense it, somehow, in my bones.

And I feel for Bathsheba, because she must be in great anguish, fearing for her life and for the life of her son.

"You know you must act, before this night is over," she says, over my silence.

Amused by how good it feels to be needed I take my time to answer. Meanwhile I am listening to my breath. It rasps strenuously in my throat.

At last, "Decisive action may be easy for a king," I tell her. "But as a father I must weigh every word I speak, because in the future it may leave a scar upon the hearts of my children."

Somewhat reluctantly she says, "I understand."

"I hope you do," say I. "They are, all of them, my flesh and blood."

"Then, act as a king," she says. "Not as a father. Name the one who will succeed you, the one who—in your judgement—may become a better ruler than the others."

I have to admit, "I have yet to make up my mind," which fills her eyes with worry. She knows all too well that Solomon, being the younger son, has less of a chance to win my favor.

"Decide," she says. "And make your wishes known. That in itself may bring about a change, a peaceful transition of power. Otherwise, I'm afraid there will be mayhem. It will start at sunrise."

I let go of her hand, because to say my next sentence I must not lean on anyone.

But before I can muster my pride, and take air in my lungs, and clear my throat to state, in my most regal tones, "I am still the king, am I not," I find myself staggering. In the next instant, there I am, a heap of arms and legs spilled on the floor, twisting in agony from the sudden chill overtaking me.

I reach up, trying to breathe her name. And I wonder what this suffering may look like, to her and to a heavenly city watching over me, floating silent and forlorn on the hill.

Overhead, a cloud breaks off from the others and moves in a new direction. Its wooly, dim grays are drifting across. I squint, rub my eyes. Now, in a separate layer, another image starts floating past: the way she looked, right here on this roof, when we came out of these doors the very first time.

I remember: scattered petals flew off, swirling in the glow around her long, silky hair that started cascading under her, onto the tile floor. In the background, a vine of roses twisted over the wooden lattice and into it. Between its diagonal slats I saw a diamond here, a diamond there of the heavens. I wondered then about the black void that was gaping upon us, dotted by a magical glint of starlight.

Separated from her by the thought of a kiss I sensed her heat, and the gust of air, which was sweetly scented by roses and by her flesh—but I could not tell if the breath between us was hers or mine. Which is when I knew, for the first time in my life, that she would always be part of my essence. I would be part of hers.

Accidentally the goblet, which she had set down next to her, tipped over and some of the wine spilled over her hip. The crisp sound of breaking glass rang in my ear. It marked the moment, from which I could not turn back. Never would I be able to put it out of my mind.

Yes, this was my fault: taking a woman that belonged to another. Soon after came the blunder: bringing her husband, Uriah, back from the front, that he may sleep with her, which would have explained her pregnancy ever so conveniently.

And when that did not go as planned, then came another mistake, the worst of all: sending him back to the battlefield, with my sealed letter in hand, arranging for his death.

All the while, my boys were learning their own lessons—not from my psalms but from my deeds. One error begets another, each one bringing a new calamity over me, over my family, and over this entire land. Sin followed by execution, followed by revolt, escape, execution, revolt...

Had I known back then the results of the results of my mistake, the curse looming over my life ever since that time, would I still choose to do it?

Bathsheba tries to raise me to my feet. Her fragrance brings back to me the sunny, warm hues of spring. The fears, the doubts flee away when we are that close. I adore the way she calls my name, the way she sighs. With every sweet word I fall deeper into her eyes.

How can love be a mistake? In my passion for her—then as now—what choice do I have?

I want to tell her, "Let me close my eyes. Let me remember."

Peace

Chapter 1

War ended that fateful day, a dozen years ago, when the king of the Ammonites was dragged before me on his knees. Once I set his magnificent crown upon my head, news spread to the neighboring nations, and they were struck with awe. All of a sudden they managed to recover something that had gone missing before: an urge to suspend all hostilities.

In the spirit of peace, their leaders came around to congratulate me on my victorious exploits. To this day they keep sending me humble greetings, written with profuse flattery, on scrolls attached to expensive gifts. Why? Perhaps to sate my appetite, so I would not find it in my heart to conquer their territories and empty their cities to fill my coffers with loot.

I often reflect on how the destruction of one place feeds the renewal of another and dread to think that a day will come—perhaps beyond my lifetime—when the City of David will stand in ruins, mourning the lives of its defenders and the exile of its few remaining men, women, and children.

I wish I could stop projecting my mind into the future or dwelling on the past. Before the change of seasons overtakes us, let me enjoy every minute of the present.

With the constant flow of goods into the land, a new era has begun. In every square, you see markets bustling with shoppers who fill their bags with imported merchandise. On every street corner, you spot buildings being erected, roofs being pitched to the happy sound of saws and hammers.

My empire stretches out all the way west to the sea, and all the way east to the wreckage, where the city of Rabbah used to stand before my conquest. That place, where the earth was drenched with blood, is now marked with an unusually vibrant burst of blossoms.

It is spring.

Seeds and potted plants arrive on special convoys to my royal gardens, and soil too, because without it they cannot take root here. With tender care, they will bloom every year from now on, opening their petals as if to let out a blood-red flame.

I find great pleasure in overseeing the renovation of my palace. It will crown the city and stand out in the center of the newly built neighborhoods as a place of gathering, where justice is to be found. I want it to become the symbol of our unity, a true gem for the entire nation.

My court is abuzz with suppliers, artisans, architects, interior designers, engineers, carpenters, brick layers, and contractors, all of them eager to win a commission from me, which makes it challenging to do my work: consult with my spiritual advisors, discuss policy matters with foreign diplomats, and exchange niceties with the elders of our tribes. I thrive on the excitement of it all.

Workers are rubbing off excess cement, which they have poured earlier across the ground, so the geometrical mosaic design starts to appear from the dirt, in all its brilliance.

Inlaid with colored glass from Tyre, trimmed on all four sides with glazed tiles from Shushan, and dotted on all four corners with shells from the delta of the Nile and pebbles from the river Tigris, this floor will create a new, vibrant ambience in my court.

A master craftsman bows deeply before me, to the point that his sketches are nearly dropping out of his portfolio.

"My lord," he says, in a heavy Egyptian accent. "Let me decorate the walls of your palace, all of them, the same way I did in the burial chambers of the pyramids."

"But," say I, "this is not a tomb."

"Too bad," he mutters, under his breath. "Unfortunately, the living are more particular about art than the dead."

"And," say I, "they're more particular about cost, too! So tell me, how much would you charge?"

He walks around the walls, measuring them by counting his paces, the better to calculate his price, which seems to annoy the worker, who is kneeling down there, a damp sponge in hand to buff the mosaic floor.

"Go away," says the worker. "Don't you dare step here, on my work!"

"It's a floor," says the master craftsman. "Isn't it?"

He comes back, hopping over the buffed areas and landing with little bows in my direction. "My lord, this court I'll do for free," he assures me, "because of your great fame, and because I'm determined to give you my very best, so I may be worthy of your generosity, which is not only known but also highly praised in our parts."

And in a lower voice he says, in an offhand manner, "Later, we'll negotiate the exact price."

"Show me your work," I demand. "You do have some sketches from your previous projects, I presume?"

Opening his portfolio, he pleads, "Here, my lord, take a look!"

Meanwhile, a merchant comes, elbowing his way towards me through a crowd of suppliers. "What these walls need is something else entirely," he says. "My finest imported rugs, which soften and even absorb the echoes in this place."

"Stop nudging me away," says the master craftsman, in a grumble.

Which the merchant seems not to hear. "Here, your majesty," he says, in a Babylonian accent, "let me spread these rugs before you—"

"Step back, both of you," the worker warns them. "The floor, it's still wet! Don't you have eyes? Can't you use them?"

Rising from my throne, "Come now," I tell the Egyptian and the Babylonian. "Let me take you to the dining hall, the reception hall, and the library. Give me your best bid. I want every space in my palace to be splashed with splendor!"

Spring it is, an awakening of all the senses, and I am indulging myself in the luxury of it all. The only place that is left as it was is my own chamber, where I keep things modest and devoid of pretense.

I like my bulky old desk, perhaps because of its grainy surface, which has been marred with a myriad of scars. Years ago, this is where my firstborn child, Amnon, carved a little face—perhaps of his half-sister, Tamar—into the wood. I remember scolding him for it, but now I cherish the touch. It brings back a memory, an old memory of how close they used to be as children.

While leading the army from one triumph to another, governing the land, and constructing a fanciful palace, a place for happiness everlasting—I have somehow missed watching him grow up. His mother, my third wife, Ahinoam of Jezreel, keeps complaining to me about it. Alas, she refuses to accept that such is the price of serving the nation.

So now, when Amnon comes into my chamber, I rise to my feet and find myself surprised to see that he is so much taller than me.

*

My boys take after me, each one in his own way, which is not always a good thing. Amnon has large, muscular hands, and to my dismay, the only thing he has learned from me is too risky: lust.

According to gossip, he is taking it to extreme, a more dangerous extreme than I could ever imagine. Perhaps that is why the two maids, who have been tidying up the sheets on my bed, exchange glances and hurry to leave the chamber as soon my son steps in.

Despite a growing unease I tell myself that the rumors must be baseless or at least exaggerated. Nothing has been proven, so there is no need to dignify idle talk by repeating it. What good will that do, besides inflaming your curiosity?

Besides, Amnon is the heir to the throne, the one to continue my legacy, so I should do everything in my power to protect his reputation.

At the same time I should allow him some latitude, some free rein. There is no harm in that, is there?

Being oblivious to his mischiefs is the only way I can hold on to my trust in him. Yet I sense that something is not quite right with him, because most of the time Amnon avoids meeting my gaze. Apparently, some thought is obsessing him. Neither one of us wants to talk about it. I find myself looking the other way.

"So," I tell him, as casually as I can, "what have you been up to lately?"

As if to dare me to a fight, he asks, "You sure you want to know?"

"Why shouldn't I?"

"Because, aren't you afraid of what people might say?"

I hesitate to ask, "What d'you mean?"

"Don't you know?" he asks, brazenly. "Don't you hear them whispering behind your back, *Like father like son*?"

"I've made my share of mistakes," I admit. "What you should learn is the lessons I took from them."

Amnon rolls his eyes, never once looking straight at me.

"Oh, stop it," he mutters. "I hate it when you lecture me, especially when you know all too well that tongues are still wagging about the scandal. I mean, your affair with that woman."

I glare at him, but it does little good when he seems to ignore it. "I've told you before," I say, sternly. "My wife has a name. Make sure you use it!"

"My mother hates her," he says, "and so do I."

I shake my head, dismayed by these petty jealousies. "Bathsheba," I say, my lips caressing the sound of her name, "has been my wife for over a dozen years now. Whatever happened before that is between me and her, and no one else. It's not for you to discuss, son. You won't understand any of it."

"Won't I," he says, not expecting an answer.

"Perhaps you would," say I, trying, for his sake, to sound agreeable. "If so, you know that a man must take control of his urges."

Amnon slaps his big hands hard upon the desk, right over that carved little face. His voice comes to a high pitch as he screeches, "So easy for you to say! You've forgotten how it feels to be young, to be consumed, burnt alive by this thing, this fire in your belly!"

To which I say, "No, not true. You may not believe me, but to this day I struggle with desire."

And he says, "Nonsense. At your age, the heat must have left you."

"But it hasn't," say I. "I'm more in love now than ever."

I find myself chuckling at the notion that my son thinks himself more virile than me. Not only am I the king but also I am known all over the empire as the greatest of lovers. I am the king of kings when it comes to expressing tenderness.

"Are you?" he asks. "Your wives used to expect a summon to your bed every night, sometimes several times a night. Now they're waiting idly, knowing that you've lost interest in them. They're preparing themselves to be doing nothing at all. There's no joining of the flesh except an occasional twiddling of thumbs."

When I an find no answer that will satisfy him, he adds, brazenly, "Perhaps that woman is to blame."

"That woman," I say, frowning at him, "has a name."

"I don't care to say it," says Amnon, with a defiant tone. "I'm told you ignore all your wives, everyone but her."

To which I say, "Stop right there! Don't you blame me—"

"Trust me," he says, baring his teeth in a smile. "I don't. Being obsessed is something I happen to understand."

I cannot deny the truth. In spite of myself I think of Bathsheba all the time, recalling the smell of her hair after the bath, and the way it would drip over my shoulders and into my hands when I kiss her. I miss the sense of intimacy between us, because lately she refuses me.

For some reason she makes herself scarce, finding excuses why she cannot come here, to my chamber. She has to take care of her child, Solomon, she says.

The boy has literary aspirations, which must be carefully nurtured, she assures me. It is time to speak with his teachers, or read his latest scribble, or check his spelling, or buy him more ink, she says.

*

Just this morning I woke up to a surprise: Bathsheba slipped into my bed, wearing a soft, silky robe that glided, ever so smoothly, off her shoulders. I knew she was in a playful mood—if you know what I mean—because of her sudden cravings.

"Strengthen me with raisins," she murmured in my ear. "Refresh me with apples, for I am faint with love."

I rushed to bring her a tray of ripe fruit. Then I put my arm around her and could not wait until she was done eating. Between one little nibble and another she told me, in her most delicious voice, to slow down.

"Do not arouse or awaken love," she said, "until it so desires."

In place of an answer I reclined back on the bed, and pointed at the blanket. I do not want to brag about it, but the fabric was stretching to a peak over me, tenting my arousal.

Just then I thought I heard someone tiptoeing just outside the chamber, in the corridor. I leapt off the bed and was surprised to find little Solomon there, his ear to the door and his hand tucked behind him, hiding something from me.

"Show me what you've got there," I said.

The kid shook his head till his freckles nearly flew of his nose. "No," he said, with a stubborn tone.

So I warned him, "I know what you've done."

His eyes widened. "You do?"

"Oh yes," said I. "You've listened to every word we said, and worse: you've written it."

"So?" He shrugs. "Is that a crime?"

"Only if you publish it."

"Not going to."

"Promise?"

"Promise."

"All the same," I insisted, "show me your hand."

Solomon raised his hand to my eyes. And just as I had expected, the palm of it was covered with minute, inky characters, spelling out the sentence, *"Do not arouse or awaken love, until it so desires."*

I peered into his innocent eyes. "You have any idea what that means?"

"Nope," said the kid. "But I'm going to figure it out. It must become clear, if I look at it long enough. Then I'll recite it out loud, before everyone—"

I cried, "You what?"

The kid smiled, and pulled his hand back. "I'll tell them things like, *'Strengthen me with raisins. Refresh me with apples, for I am faint with love.'* People find me adorable when they hear me say such words."

"They what?"

"They say it's pure poetry. They say I take after you, daddy! So it doesn't really matter, does it, if I don't get what exactly it all means—they will!"

"But, but," I stammer, "these aren't your words! They belong to your mom and me!"

"Don't worry," said Solomon. "I won't tell them that."

Straddling between anger and an undeniable sense of amusement I wagged my finger at him.

"Go wash your hand at once," I said. "What we talk about, your mom and I, isn't meant for your ears. It's private."

"Nope," he said. "Once I write it down, it's mine."

"Isn't," said I.

Having closed the door I climbed back into bed.

Holding an apple in her hand Bathsheba offered me a bite and said, "Who was that?"

"Oh, no one," said I. "Now, where were we?"

"Don't you know?" she said, and in her soft, melodious voice, she started humming to me, between one kiss and another. "*Kiss me, David, with the kisses of your mouth, for your love is more delightful than wine.*"

I was about to tell her we must keep it down. Instead I loosened her robe and while caressing her I hummed back, "*I will go to the mountain of myrrh, and to the hill of incense. You are altogether beautiful, my darling, there is no flaw in you.*"

Bathsheba smiled, and over my murmur she went on singing, "*No wonder the young women love you! Take me away with you, let us hurry!*"

"Oh yes," said I. "Let us hurry."

*

Amnon claims that obsession is one thing he understands, but of course I cannot tell him any of that, can I? Instead, thinking myself a caring father, I try to turn his attention to other things, to his future.

"You are the heir to the throne," I remind him. "Aren't you the least bit interested in matters of the state?"

"No," he says, with a shrug. "The office has no charm for me."

"Really?" I ask, a bit surprised by this apparent lack of ambition. "Why, are you worried that to govern, you may need to sacrifice your conscience?"

"I have none of that," he says, plainly. "And I know nothing at all about sacrifice. What was the question, again?"

For a while I allow silence to form between us.

Then, "Forget it," I tell him. "I must have misunderstood you."

"Did you ever understand me?" he asks, raising an eyebrow.

And when I hold myself back from a sharp reply Amnon bursts out laughing. "You have no idea who I am! Perhaps it's better this way."

"You're my son, my successor," I announce. "Leadership is a skill, with the right tools it can be honed—"

"It's a dull thing, for me," he says, cutting in. "And dull it shall always remain. Besides I don't want to hear how great you are, and how grateful I should be to bask in your majestic presence. And certainly I don't need your wise advice."

With an indignant tone I say, "Have I ever said anything close to that to you?"

In reply he quotes one of my many proverbs, making a mockery out of it. "*Listen, my son, to your father's instruction and do not forsake your mother's teaching. They are a garland to grace your head and a chain to adorn your neck.*"

"What's wrong with that?"

"I don't want to be chained."

"I see," say I. "Forget the chain. Forget the garland, too. Prepare yourself for the crown."

"I'll never be anointed," he says, crossly. "Odds are against me."

"How, how can you think that?" I stammer. "You're my firstborn! By the law of the land you shall, without a doubt, become the next king of Israel. If you wish I can teach you—"

"You've taught me well enough, already," he says, curling his lips slyly.

"Really? Have I?"

"In every legend, every old folk's tale I've heard from you, surprise! It's always the youngest son who—against all expectations—gets the position of authority over his brothers."

At that I cannot help but smile. "True, such was the case when, in the presence of my older brothers, I was anointed by old prophet Samuel. He chose me to succeed—"

"My point exactly," cries Amnon. "Don't you get it? Being the eldest in this family I'm already at a disadvantage!"

And before I can open my mouth, or even think of a way to retort, he adds, "Stop telling me, then, about the law of the land. Who cares about it!"

"Don't even joke about it," say I, giving him a look. "When you rule, the law is meant to be obeyed, which is why I make sure it's carved in stone."

"Until then," he says, "it's meant to be broken."

And to himself he hisses, "Such nonsense. Law, carved in stone? Maybe in those dreary old times! Nowadays it's scribbled on papyrus, which is an entirely different thing. What the hell does he know?"

Having children is a way for life to humble you. Even so I find myself surprised to be treated as if I were ignorant, unfamiliar with new methods, and worst of all, out of touch with the young. No, I tell myself, that cannot be—but before I can convince myself otherwise, there is a soft knock at my door.

She leans in, a bright spark in her eyes.

"Come in," I tell my daughter, opening my arms to her. "Give me a kiss, Tamar."

Mocking my greeting by repeating it in his own, somewhat sickening manner, Amnon says, "Yeah, you heard him. Give it to us!"

She takes one look at her half-brother and steps back cautiously, so as to avoid inflaming that desire, that obsession of his. From the depth of the corridor she gives me a quick, dimpled smile, and disappears.

*

I have been blessed with many treasures, none more precious than my daughter. Her mother, Maachah, daughter of Talmai, king of Geshur, chose the name Tamar, which suggested to her the honeyed sweetness of dates.

The name brought back to me a historical figure, without whom my tribe, the tribe of Judah, would never have come into existence. To this day I have never shared with my daughter the legendary courage of her namesake. Perhaps the time has come for me to tell her the story. She will cherish it.

With this in mind I take leave of Amnon and head downstairs, to the women's quarters. The door is slightly ajar. At first glance, the place seems vacant. Afternoon light is flying in through the arched windows, setting the curtains aglow.

Rays are slanting down onto the marble floor, and from there they are bouncing upward onto the opposite wall, which is decorated with embroidered panels. And there, at the far end of the space, I spot two figures.

My fourth wife, Maachah, is standing there with her back to me. Her matronly figure is clad in a dark, shapeless dress. She takes a step back from our daughter to adore her fragile beauty, the golden fuzz glimmering like a halo around her hair, the innocence shining in her eyes.

Then my wife moves closer to Tamar, gathering a silky garment around her slender waist, measuring here, mending there, making sure it will be a good fit. It is a coat of many colors, richly ornamented with minute, sparkling gems, as becomes a virgin princess, a daughter of mine.

Peeking in through the half open door I ask myself, How did Tamar grow up so fast? At this moment she is no longer a girl, nor is she a woman, yet—but she is, and always will be, my baby.

I still remember the first time I held her.

The ghost of her crib is still registered in my mind. It used to stand right there, under the ruffled edge of that curtain. How can I forget: she gurgled, trying to fix her eyes on me, curious to see, to separate me out of what to her must have seemed like a dim mess. I saw myself reflected in her pupils. Her world back then was nothing but blurry shapes.

The tiny hands flailed about in the air, fingering it delicately, as if to find out who was standing above her, whispering, "Oh, little one, this seems like chaos to me, too."

I picked up the precious little bundle and rocked her gently, back and forth, forth and back. I brushed my lips around her scalp, careful not to touch the tender spot, right there at the top. The fine fuzz of her hair tickled my nose, which brought me, at once, to a sneeze.

Fourteen years later I think I know what to expect. Princes from kingdoms near and far will soon arrive here to compete for her hand. Many political alliances will be forged during their visit, which should please me. Instead it makes me irate. Let them wait.

Let this moment linger just a little while longer. Let me savor it. This is a time of promise, a time of peace. We are safe. For the first time in history there is no threat from outside. Even so I vow, one more time, to protect her from all trouble, come what may.

I have been too busy, far too long. I need more time to get to know the young woman she is becoming. I wonder what she is thinking right now, what words cross her mind as she is standing there, in quiet anticipation, her coat of many colors almost ready, almost touched by the light.

With her charm Tamar is poised to exceed the fame of her legendary namesake. No need to tell her outdated stories, when her future is here, waiting.

The Plot

Chapter 2

This morning things start on a bad note and go worse from there. My fourth wife, Maachah, catches sight of me doing my best to resolve some financial dispute between two merchants, which she interprets as ignoring her. Naturally she stamps her foot, which—to her delight—leaves a dent on the freshly installed mosaic floor.

If that is not bad enough she interrupts me, for no better reason than to point out, once again, that she comes from royalty, whereas I come from a family of lowly shepherds, which means I must listen to her, because now, right now is the time to give our daughter away—or else.

So I say, "Or else, what?"

And she says, in her Geshurite accent, "Or else, Tamar will become an old maid, heaven forbid! You don't want that, now do you?"

When I shrug Maachah leaves, not before stamping her foot again. After that, she enlists an ally, the one man she knows will annoy me—one way or another—into giving in to her whims. This arguably valuable talent belongs to none other than my old adviser, Nathan.

When he comes before me I turn away at once, to avoid looking at his beard. Its feathery strands come to a tip, which reminds me of a goat. I almost expect him to inspect the new polish on the furniture by nibbling at it, or at least brushing his upper lip and tongue against it.

Nathan speaks sheepishly, at first.

"I suggest," he says, in his quivering voice, "that you listen to your wife—"

Merely for the sake of precision I ask, "Which one of them?"

He knows that I know the answer, which is why he ignores my question. "Why not consider these foreign suitors?" he asks. "They've already sent their greetings, with gold coins that bear their image, so your daughter can get an idea, well ahead of their visit, of how good they look when embossed."

"What?" I cry, in alarm. "They're coming here? Who invited them?"

Nathan cups his hand around his ear, pretending to be hard of hearing, which allows him to go on to say, "Why don't you check out the coins? Sort them out by their weight, and choose the best candidate! Each one of them represents a unique opportunity, a political deal that can be sealed—the sooner the better—with a marriage."

To postpone my answer I shrug. "Who am I to decide?"

And he says, as if I needed to be reminded, "Why, you're the king!"

I flip my scepter in the air, for lack of knowing what exactly should be done with the thing. Then I catch it and ask, "Shouldn't my daughter be the one to make up her own mind?"

"Why would she?" he asks, as if this was an unheard of proposition. "She's just a girl—"

"That's exactly the point!"

"I don't get it, your majesty—"

"Like you said, Tamar is just a girl. She's young, pure of heart, and much too immature to be betrothed, especially to someone she barely even knows."

Nathan utters a sigh. "If not for her purity, d'you think they would be coming here to woo her? It's so hard these days to find brides from good homes, let alone virgin brides! My God," he says, clapping a hand over his chest. "What's the world coming to?"

"Oh, stop it! I don't want to talk about marriages, not now," I say, and for added emphasis I wag my scepter at him.

Which makes him change direction, only to end up heading for the same place.

"Let's talk about something else, then. Politics?" he asks, taking my silence to mean what he wants it to mean. "Tell me: what's wrong with arranging your alliances to your advantage?"

"Not at the cost of letting my little princess go, before she's ready for it," say I, trying to resist a sudden urge to take hold of his long, woolly ear and twist it this way and that between my thumb and forefinger, till he bleats.

"History repeats itself," he bleats. "Why, her mother, Maachah, was her father's little princess too, yet he sent her here, to marry you."

To which I say, "As I recall, he was all too happy to shove her into my arms."

"Oops," says Nathan, as if he has just stepped into a trap. "Any complaints about her?"

"No, not really," say I. "I enjoy her, for the most part! And I trust she enjoys me, too—except for the numerous occasions when she drones on and on, telling me how sweet she is and how I must prove, time and time again, that I adore her for it, by lavishing expensive gifts upon her, or else."

"Or else, what?"

"She's going to tell on me."

"To whom?"

"To her daddy, of course, king Talmai of Geshur."

"I thought he's your ally."

"He is," I say, "as long as she has nothing to complain about, which is rarely the case. If nothing else, she tells him, 'The people in this place—all of them but me—speak with a foreign accent.' Oh, how I wish I could send her back to his territory, where she wouldn't have to suffer so much, in an effort to twist her tongue around what she calls, 'The harsh sounds of that horribly primitive language!'"

"You can't send her back," says Nathan. "That would cause an international crisis."

"But," say I, "it would make my life a lot simpler."

He rolls his eyes to heaven.

I wish to find some excuse to leave him to his prayers. So imagine my relief when a servant rushes in, wearing a long, worried face, to tell me that an urgent matter needs my attention.

"What is it?" I demand, barely able to contain my joy—only to see it evaporate at once.

"Forgive me," says the servant. "I'm sorry, your majesty, so sorry to bring you bad news. Your firstborn, Amnon, has been stricken with something, some mysterious illness."

*

At hearing this news I am greatly alarmed, because it is rather unusual for my children to fall ill. All of them are blessed with excellent health, with a single exception: Bathsheba's first son, who died within days of his birth, because of me.

Grief comes back to haunt me every time I conjure that moment, thirteen years ago, when I leaned over his crib to take a last look at him. His tiny body was already stiffening, his face —pale. A single ray of sun cut across his ashen cheek, leaving his eyes in the shadows.

So now, with a heavy feeling in my heart, I rush out of the court and without waiting for my chariot to be brought for me I run down the hill to see Amnon.

Upon entering his house I find myself confused—even before taking a look at him—to see that things in it have been staged in a new manner. Perhaps it just seems that way, because of the remarkably dim air, which is thick with some medicinal vapor. It blots the outlines of the furniture, and casts gloom over the entire space. The heavy cabinet that used to stand opposite the bedroom door is now barricading it, so I have to find my way around that obstacle.

Usually at this hour the windows are wide open, so sunlight may pour in, to showcase the bed in all its decadence. It is an expensive, heavy piece, decorated according to his taste, with fancy inlays of metal, mother-of-pearl, and ivory, contrasting each other in hue and shine. But now, the thing is drenched in shadows.

In the dark, you barely note the life-sized statue of a nude holding a fan, standing at this corner of the bed, and the matching statue at the other corner. Carved of Egyptian alabaster, both of these figures lean forward as if to stop you right there, and prevent you from slipping around them. I imagine that if not for being suspended in that motion, they would hiss something, some sordid secret in your ear.

The scarlet draperies have been pulled shut, allowing only a single ray of sun to wander in, and reach for the pillow. There lies Amnon, having dropped his hand limply, and perhaps a bit theatrically, over the edge of the mattress.

As if threatening to cross him off, the blade of light rests there, barely stirring across his cheek, which brings back the old grief. Tears well in my eyes, stinging me. I blink them off and try to find Amnon's eyes, but they are obscure to me, completely hidden in the deepest shadow. Perhaps I have yet to adjust to the dark.

"I'm so hot," he sighs, his voice husky. "Oh, am I in fever!"

I climb the carpeted stairs to his bed, which is not an easy thing to do, aided only by a sense of touch—but before I can reach the top, someone steps in from behind the nude statue.

Startled I look up at this man.

"Your majesty," he says, over the voice of my son, who is moaning and groaning up there. "I didn't startle you, did I? This is me, Jonadab, son of your brother Shimeah."

To which I mutter, "I know who you are."

My nephew is known to be a shrewd man. I value his counsel, yet do not want to hear it, because there are too many advisors in my employ already. I am tired of getting too much advice, much of which is often conflicting.

I recall that Jonadab submitted an application to join my team of advisors, which I declined. Of late he has found his way to Amnon and now, apparently, he serves as his confidant.

Right now he wears a decidedly grave countenance, which is interrupted, from time to time, by a sly, quick smirk.

"I wish," he says, "that I could meet you under happier circumstances. I had no choice but to send for you, because as you can see, your son is sick."

As if to prove him right Amnon tosses the bedsheets away, so I can see the beads of sweat on his half-naked body. His head lolling to one side of the pillow, he mumbles, "I'm on fire! I'm burning alive!"

I raise my hand to his forehead—but before I can feel it, Jonadab claps his hand over my wrist.

"Your majesty, no! Don't touch!" he says, his voice spiking into fright. "It's best to keep a distance from him."

And noting my puzzled look, he explains, "I've already sent for the best doctors in the city. None of them has a clue. They can't even begin to guess what ails your son. So I advise you, your majesty: be cautious. "

Meanwhile Amnon keeps crying, in a babyish tone, "Oh, I'm hot, hot, hot!"

Jonadab leans over him and whispers something in his ear, as if to quiet him.

Then, with a twist of a smile, he turns back to me and says, suggestively, "Alas, sickness has a way of reducing even a grown man to his knees, so he may behave like a newborn. Look at him. Doesn't he look like one?"

I look at Amnon, surprised to note that his skin has a healthy glow, but then what do I know? If the doctors have given up on him, how can I doubt their opinion?

I press my hands against my temples, and feel the tears beginning to stream down my face. I find myself drowned in their bitter taste, and in despair. How much must I sacrifice to sate this God, this unseen power that plays so carelessly with my life, and with the lives of my children? Is He coming back to exact a punishment upon my house, targeting not me—but another one of them?

Would it be Amnon this time? Would he have to pay for my sin?

"Because by doing this you have shown utter contempt for the Lord," Nathan told me back then, before the birth of my baby, "the son born to you shall die."

"Oh, help me," cries Amnon. "Help me, father."

Meanwhile the blade of light has rolled along the flesh. It is now pointing at the tip of his thumb. His hand—large, tan, and packed with muscle—seems to be trembling, which in a blink, brings to mind the fragile hand of Bathsheba's baby, dying.

I remember how the glow touched the tips of his tiny, nearly transparent fingers, how delicately it revealed something new in them, a sudden paralysis.

When illuminated this way, the memory becomes unbearable to me. "What I can do?" I whisper.

Which is the moment Amnon stops moaning. To my surprise he props himself up, and leans his head upon the carved headrest, even though Jonadab tries to hint to him that he should be lying flat.

"Tell me," I plead. "How can I help?"

Hugging his scarlet pillow with both arms Amnon says, plaintively, "You know I haven't eaten for three days now."

What can I say, but this, "I believe you, son. Shall I call for the cook to bring you a meal, specially made to revive you? What would you like?"

"No," he says, exchanging a quick glance with the other. "I can't bring myself to eat."

"Eat you must," I insist, "to restore yourself to health."

He shakes his head. "You can see for yourself. I'm too weak. Can't do anything by myself."

So I offer, "I'll get someone to feed you."

Amnon chortles behind his hand, or perhaps he coughs, I cannot tell which. In the dimness I spot a flash, the sudden flash of his canine teeth.

"In that case," he says, hungrily now, "I'd like my sister Tamar to come and—"

"She should come," Jonadab weaves his words in, as if he knows the script for the plot, as if he is the one spinning it. "She should make him some food—"

"She should make me her dumplings," says Amnon, passing his tongue over the red, plump lips. "Right here in my sight, so I may eat from her soft, dimpled hand."

Was that a lustful glint in his eye?

No, I tell myself, that cannot be. The light here must be playing a trick on me. Rebellious as he may be Amnon would never play a joke on me, especially not this way, conspiring with someone else to make me a fool.

And even if he would I trust my instinct to warn me in time. I have lived by my wits my entire life, and have always relied on my ability to read those around me, and penetrate their minds. My son is no different. He cannot be, can he?

He is my firstborn, the one I am bound to trust, above all others. There is nothing I will withhold from him, especially now, when he is so weak, so susceptible. Besides, even if I'm making a mistake, what's the worst that can happen?

I ask for a quill so as to write a note to Tamar. Jonadab has it right there, at the ready. It has been neatly sharpened, so as not to waste any time.

"Come to the house of your brother Amnon," I tell her in my note, "and prepare some food for him." I consider for a moment if I should replace the word *food* with *dumpling*. I decide against it, perhaps because for me, it evokes the unpleasant sight of Amnon licking his lips.

And so, without delay, the note is sealed and on its way.

Assault
Chapter 3

The conversation with Amnon keeps haunting me as I climb uphill, back to my palace. I find his last question disturbing, without being able to explain why.

It seemed innocent enough, at first. "Would you do anything for me?"

To which I said, "Of course, son."

"How much are you willing to sacrifice?"

"What kind of a question is that?"

In place of an answer, he pressed on. "Would you become my accomplice?"

"To do what?" I wondered, because no crime had been named. I mean, his mind is far from being transparent! How was I supposed to guess what he was thinking about?

Amnon fanned his half-naked body with the untucked edge of his bedsheets, and turned the conversation to something else.

"This is fun, seeing you sitting here, in my company," he said.

To which I said, "So did I. We should do it more often."

"Remember what you lectured me," he asked, "over and over again?"

"What's that, son?"

"You said, '*Blessed is the one who does not walk in step with the wicked, or stand in the way that sinners take, or sit in the company of mockers.*"

"I remember," said I.

Then, hissing at me Amnon asked, "You feel blessed, father? Do you?"

It is not until I emerge from the woods and enter the clearing, just ahead of the entrance to the courtyard, that my eyes finally adjust to the brilliant sunlight. It is with that clarity that I challenge myself. I ask, over and over, "Why, why did I send Tamar to his house?"

And I defend myself by asking, time and again, "So what if I sent her to him? What's the worst that can happen?"

And time and again I reply, "Nothing, really, not a thing," only to find myself less and less confident of my answer.

Those thick vapors, and the pungent smell of medicine in his chamber must have confounded me, somehow, into believing him. But now I grasp what should have been obvious to me from the beginning. My son is not sick, not really.

True, he is consumed by some thought, obsessed to the point of agony, but his body seemed strong enough, despite the beads of sweat—or was it merely water, that had been sprinkled with great abundance all over him, and over his bedsheets. He could not have fooled me better if he were wearing a mask.

My son is not in sickness—but sick in his craft.

If not for my own obsession—recalling the sight of Bathsheba's baby, dying—I might have been able to realize, much earlier, that I am being played for a fool.

Amnon knows me. He knows how vulnerable I can become, given the right circumstances. As a child, he may have witnessed how I stood over the crib, where the little one had stopped crying, how distraught I was by that sudden silence.

And that blade of light that rested upon the baby, that must have left an impression, not only on my memory but also on my son's memory. How else can you explain the precision with which he staged the scene in his house. Every word must have been rehearsed, every gesture—practiced. All of it was designed—perhaps too perfectly—to bring back my grief and let me drown in it all over again.

I enter my court and pace like a madman around it. Is Amnon merely feigning his sickness? If so, I tell myself, there is nothing sinister about it, is there not?

I did worse than that in my youth. I mean, I feigned madness in the court of Achish, king of the city of Gath, for no better reason than to convince the Philistines that I posed no danger to them, so they would let me stay alive.

Pretending to be insane came easy for me. After all I had learned from the best, having worked such a long time in the court of a madman.

I remember: there I was, in the hands of the Philistines, so what choice did I have but to act like a lunatic? With my fingernails I scratched at the walls, and made marks on the doors of the gate, all the while letting saliva run down my beard.

I remember: they went on making fun of me, so I figured I might as well join their performance.

So I broke into their midst, hopped onto the center of the hearth, and kicked its pebbles till they flew out every which way.

Then I sang with bold ecstasy at the utmost top of my voice, "David! David! David!" and pointed my fingers, glaring at everyone around me. And for a grand finale I rolled my eyeballs around in their sockets, and let out a terrifying wail, which silenced each and every one of them.

Alas, it took the wind out of me, so I fell to the floor, where I started convulsing, with just enough breath to let my lips twitch.

They cupped their ears, bending over me to listen. I wheezed, "Saul has killed his thousands, and David his tens of thousands... Tens of thousands... Tens of thousands..." And with spasm, again I cried, "David! David! David!"

I flattered myself into believing that no one comes close to me, and that my skill for acting is unmatched. How vain, how misguided I was, how great was my folly! Now I wonder, has Amnon inherited my talent? Has he perfected it, somehow, beyond anything I could have imagined? His performance, a few hours ago, must have amused him immensely, at my expense.

I am the fool—but he is the one deserving a round of applause!

And his confidant, Jonadab, is clever indeed. Cleverly has he directed him, guided his hand. All Amnon had to do was make it tremble, ever so slightly, when the light rolled upon it, and then wait, wait just a little bit for my emotions to overtake me, blunt my judgement, and serve his purpose.

The only question that torments me now is this: what could his purpose be? Let me rephrase it: what have I become an accomplice to, unwittingly? What is the crime—

And the minute I ask it, the answer becomes clear, dreadfully clear to me. My heart starts hammering, hammering heavily inside my chest. I try to calm myself with a memory of the old days, when for the first time I held my newborn daughter in my arms.

It was then that an incredible thing happened: Tamar not only looked at me but also her eyes widened, and for the first time she saw me, and wrapped her transparent little fingers around my thumb. Now her mouth opened into the sweetest, loveliest smile, and she cooed at me in recognition.

I had never experienced anything like this moment before. Overwhelmed by happiness I felt the pounding of her heart next to mine. It was then that I made a solemn vow: I would become the best father ever, and protect her, then and in the future, from all trouble.

Now I rush out of the court to stop what I know is about to happen. A horde of servants forms around me, which unfortunately slows me down. They are crossing each other in great confusion, running every which way, unsure what I want, what is expected of them, and why there is such a wild, frightened look in my eyes.

"Beware," cries one of them, pointing at the horizon. "Look: the sky is darkening."

"A storm is coming," cries another.

And a third one begs me, "Come back into the palace, your majesty! This is a dangerous time to be outdoors."

I pay no attention to them, and without waiting for my stable boy to bridle my stallion I mount it.

I tap my heels into its sides, urging the animal first into trotting, then into galloping at a blistering pace down the hill to my son's house. I can no longer deny knowing the desire that ails him, nor can I pretend to doubt the rumors. Lately, they have become wild, and far too persistent. Amnon has forced himself on young girls before. I've heard of it. I know it.

Now can I get there in time, before he lays a hand on my only daughter?

Blood throbbing. Veins swelling. Heart coming close to a burst. Rage. Then, a sudden gust of wind slaps my face. Blustering in from the east, a hot, howling gale whips desert sand into the air, blinding me.

I blink away the dust, the tears, and charge ahead, riding my stallion at full speed, nearly slipping over the acorns strewn all over, under the oak trees. Hooves drumming, drumming upon the dirt road, never fast enough.

As I turn the bend I spot a dark figure racing ahead opposite me through the woods. For a minute I think I see myself—a reflection of me in him. There is that young man, flying through the gap between one tree trunk and another, coming at me through the next gap, and the one after that. He crosses my path and blocks me. So I rein in my stallion, and when the dust settles I recognize him.

There, against a background of tortuous, thorny branches, sitting astride his mule, is my second son, Absalom.

He is Tamar's brother, and like her, he is slender, shorter than his half-brother, Amnon, and utterly magnificent to behold— even when his nostrils flare, even when he fumes at me, such as right now. Blow after blow, his hair rises around him in the ferocious wind. His jaw is set. Glaring at me, his bright eyes are ablaze.

Something—I cannot tell what it is, at first—drops down out of his fist. It flutters down, all the way to the ground, like a wounded dove. Absalom grips the hilt of his sword, pulls it smoothly out of its sheath, and bends over to pierce the crumpled thing. Then he lifts it from the dirt with the sharp tip and points it at my eyes.

"Is this your handwriting?" he demands.

I rub my eyes to remove the grit and look at the note, which I have written earlier that day, barely able to recognize my own letters. In my haste, the ink must have bled over them. I pray that like me, Tamar could not decipher what I asked of her.

"Is this your handiwork? Is it?" he cries, over the shrieking wind.

In place of an answer I hang my head in shame.

"I see," he says. "Where is she?"

I am too confused to give an answer, and to my relief he avoids pressing me for it. Instead he turns the mule around.

It comes from an interesting breed, having inherited from its sire the donkey's trait of sure-footedness, and from its dam—the mare's trait of speed, both of which will serve it well on its way down this slope. Absalom rubs the neck of the animal, as if to praise it, and to me he says, tersely, "How I've admired you, father! How I trusted you—until today."

And in an instant he is gone.

I follow the clip-clop of the hooves around the bend and down the hill, aching to arrive already, to find my daughter and rock her softly in my arms, as if she were still a baby.

These are the words I would sing to her, this is the promise I would make: *"The city of Tyre will come with a gift, people of wealth will seek your favor. All glorious is the princess within her chamber, her gown interwoven with gold."*

But when at last I reach Amnon's house, the place seems deserted—except for an old maidservant who acts as if she were deaf. She would not answer any of my questions, my pleas. Head hanging over a washbasin, she is bent on scrubbing the scarlet bedsheets, trying to rub away a large stain of blood.

"Where's Tamar?" I ask, in a voice that is thick with worry. "And Amnon? You seen him? Where's he?"

She waves her dripping hand at me, but it is unclear if this is meant to indicate that there is no one inside—or that I, too, should leave the place.

I shout at her, hearing my voice echo, with great urgency, throughout the house, "Your master, Amnon, where's he?"

The maidservant brings a finger to her wrinkled lips, perhaps to calm me down, which is when, for the first time, I start listening. Like me, she cups her ear. There is a sound out there, barely human—but somehow I recognize that it is not the wind, wailing with such despair, such sad lament.

At last, "There. There she is," the maidservant whispers, breaking her silence.

"Tamar?" I say, hoping the answer would be No.

"Tamar," she says, her voice cracking. "I was told to do it."

"Do what?"

"Was it my fault? My job is to obey orders."

"What was it you did?"

I can barely hear her, as she says, "I had no choice but to put her out and bolt the door shut after her. She was wearing an ornate coat, a coat of many colors, the kind of garment virgin princesses would wear. Once she found herself on the street Tamar ripped it. She put ashes on her head and put her hands on her head and went away, weeping aloud as she went."

*

That evening, after hours of searching for her all over the city—climbing to the top of the Mount of Olives, down to the Valley of Kidron, around Mount Scorpius, along the Valley of Hinnom, all the while following those faint, illusive wails that echoed between one rock and another, all around me—I find myself exhausted.

Later, in my chamber, I am unable to fall asleep. As long as I stay awake, the same day is still here, and my daughter is missing only since its morning.

In spite of the late hour I go down to the court and spend several hours there, interrogating each and every one of my son's servants, as well as witnesses who might have seen her wondering the streets of Jerusalem. Long after midnight I dismiss them and drag my feet up the stairs, back to my chamber. I find myself in a daze, staring blankly at Goliath's sword, which is hung opposite me, on the wall.

From this distance, it seems small, and the victory I gained in that battle—easy. What a delightful game it was, to figure out my opponent! By comparison, peacetime is more tricky, as the enemy is unknown. He may come from within, from your own family. He may be your own flesh and blood. If you kill him, part of you is bound to die.

Sitting down I lay my head upon the desk. By the touch I know: here is my daughter's face, which my child, Amnon, carved into the wooden surface years ago, when she was a newborn baby. Perhaps this scar is all that remains of a happier time.

Perhaps this is all there is.

One thing is obvious: what happened today behind closed doors between Amnon and Tamar should be blotted out. I must instruct my court historians to avoid investigating it, let alone writing it for posterity. This story should remain out of their records. Why, then, do I feel compelled to sharpen my quill? I have no answer, except this: if I write everything down and then read it back to myself, perhaps I will find a way to make sense of it all.

Confusion makes me uneasy. Then again, in this case it may be less painful than clarity. Perhaps it is better to knock the inkwell upside down and let the ink bleed across my characters, obscuring them completely.

The twists and turns of the assault have been relayed to me by the servants who were all listening, cowering behind the door, taking turns to watch through the keyhole. As I recall their voices, the tip of my feather hovers over the blank leather scroll. Of its own, it starts its journey at the slant of the first letter, writing:

So Tamar went to the house of her half-brother Amnon, who was lying down. She took some dough, kneaded it, made the dumplings in his sight and cooked them.

I imagine she could feel the obsession, the weight of his gaze at her back, as he was taking in every single one of her movements. As tension grew between them, she must have spotted the glint, the flareup of lust, escaping from the corner of his eye every now and again.

Still Tamar resisted the urge to leave, because she respected my command and made up her mind to be obey it. She would be brave, even to her own detriment. Besides, she figured that Amnon was of no danger, because he was sick, was he not? And as long as there were servants around her Amnon would have to restrain himself.

At least for the moment Tamar was safe.

Then she took the pan and set it before him, but he refused to eat.
"Send everyone out of here," Amnon said.
Faithfully did Jonadab do his bidding.. "Out, all of you!" he shouted,
avoiding to look at Tamar, who turned pale.
And so, everyone but her left the chamber.

I imagine that she asked herself if she should leave, too, but held herself firm. Still, she respected my command.

Perhaps she recalled the story, the old fable about Joseph who sent all his Egyptian servants out of the room, so he might make himself known to his own brothers, who had sold him into slavery.

Tamar must have trusted that in the same manner, Amnon wanted to make himself known to her. Which he used to his advantage, because this was his chance, if you get what I mean, to know her.

Then Amnon told her, "Bring the food here into my bedroom so I may eat from your hand."

So Tamar took the dumplings she had prepared and brought them to him in his bedroom.

Under his breath he said, "Those dimples on you, they drive me out of my mind."

She turned to go, which was when he grabbed her arm and said, "Come to bed with me, my sister."

"No, my brother!" she said. "Don't force me! Such a thing should not be done in Israel! Don't do this wicked thing."

In place of an answer Amnon shoved his elbow into her soft belly.

Which flooded her eyes with tears. "What about me?" she pleaded. "Where would I be able to get rid of my disgrace?"

"You can only blame yourself," he said, gruffly, "for tempting me so."

Not one of the servants, who were watching Amnon and Tamar through the keyhole, dared to confront their master, so as to give her a chance, an opening to escape. And so, there she was, left to fend for herself.

As I write the words I find myself amazed by my daughter, not only her courage but also her wits. How eloquently she tried to reason with him, caution him of the results of his actions, pointing them out so he may see them from his point of view:

"And what about you?" she asked, trying to reason with him, even as he thrust his knee into her legs, to subdue her. "You would be like one of the wicked fools in Israel."

With a single rip Amnon tore off her garment, that lovely coat of many colors.

Realizing that help would not come, and that she is too frail to hold him off, "Please," said Tamar. "Do things the right way. Speak to the king. He will not keep me from being married to you."

But Amnon refused to listen. Being stronger than her, he slapped his hand across her face, holding her mouth shut, and he raped her.

The tip of my feather has slowed to a grind. It can barely move now, because here comes the worst, most heart-rending part:

Then Amnon hated her with intense hatred. In fact, he hated her more than he had loved her.
He said, "Get up and get out!"
"No," said Tamar. She had become a woman, raped. If he would not marry her, no one else would. "Sending me away would be a greater wrong than what you have already done to me."
But he refused to listen, because to him this was not about fairness, not even about passion. It was about power. Having broken her, he would throw her out.
Without giving her another look, Amnon called his servant and with utter despise he said, "Get this woman out of my sight, and bolt the door after her."

*

All night long, the wind has been raging outside. Only now, at sunrise, does it subside, turning into sighs.

I wake up to soft footfalls, approaching me from behind.

"Who's here?" I ask, raising my head from the hard surface of the desk.

In place of an answer Bathsheba kisses my daughter's face, which is carved into it, and with the same gentle sweep, she touches her lips to my forehead.

"Tamar," she tells me, "has been found."

"Oh, at last! When is she coming home?"

"She isn't. She wouldn't."

"Why would she," I whisper. "It's all my fault."

As swiftly as she has come, Bathsheba turns to leave the chamber, not before telling me, with tender pity in her voice, "Give her time, David."

"She'll never come back. I know it."

"In a few weeks, when Tamar has recovered a bit, I'll ask her again," says Bathsheba. "I promise."

I grip my head in both hands.

"What's the point of asking," I say out loud, to no one in particular. "From now on Tamar will stay away from me. I've betrayed her."

There is nothing I can do, except this: roll the sheet of leather, to which I have committed her story, and hide it under a pile of maps and notes in a deepest drawer of my desk, so no one will ever find it.

Then I turn back to Bathsheba, hoping she has not noticed what I have just done—or else I will have to contend with something that is craftier than me: a woman's curiosity.

But no. Instead of asking questions Bathsheba says, simply, "Come here, David."

I come. We hold each other, but my mind wonders.

Having failed to protect Tamar, I must shield her now in an entirely different way. No one should learn these sordid details of the assault. In public, the story should be denied, if at all possible. For certain, it should not make it into the official records of history, because that would be like violating my daughter all over again.

Be Quiet for Now

Chapter 4

In the wake of the brutal attack upon my daughter I feel a pressing need to keep up appearances, and so does my second son, Absalom. I am told that he said to his sister, Tamar, "Has that Amnon, your brother, been with you?"

She covered her mouth with both hands to overcome a sob, and her whole body shook uncontrollably.

"Be quiet for now, my sister," said Absalom. "He's your brother. Don't take this thing to heart."

Really? Don't take this thing to heart? I worry about him, because he may give her this advice, yet—like me—he is unable to follow it.

You can see the fire in his eyes. Absalom is burning from within, seething with rage, because his sister has been disgraced. Every time he happens to cross paths with his half-brother, Amnon—in the palace or in the royal gardens—there is blood on his lips, because he bites them, bites as hard as he can, so as not to say a word, not a single word, good or bad.

"Be quiet," he must be telling himself. "For now."

His is a strange silence, a massive one. As days turn to weeks and weeks grow into months, it keeps expanding. On what note will it end?

Lately Absalom avoids not only his half-brother but also me. Sometimes I wish he would scream, because then I could join him in his sorrow, and grieve for the pain, for the loss of innocence for my daughter, and for the unrest amongst all my children. Perhaps then we could come out at the other side of this agony, and start healing.

But for now, waiting for me to avenge her rape, he is quiet.

I should do something to reach out to him. I know I should. But a change has come upon me, which my court scribes, Nathan the prophet and Gad the Seer, note even before I do. In the past I had to explain my actions to them. I never thought I would miss those days. Now, for the sake of history, they want to understand about the opposite thing: my lack of action.

I cannot deal with their questions. They make me feel trapped, confounded into muteness.

Bending his wiry figure before me Nathan bleats into my right ear, "Why, why don't you hold Amnon responsible?"

Gad bends before me in a like fashion. He wears the same cloth-sack, perhaps to suggest that he, too, is a man of God, and should be revered, too, for all that praying and fasting. With the same plaintive tone he bleats into my left ear, "Why, why don't you punish him for what he's done?"

Their wispy goat beards are tickling me left and right. Before long they may start sniffing me and nibbling on my ears. So I get up from the throne, climb off the stage, and pace around the court away from both of them.

I pretend to be busy with some pressing matter of state, such as how one might handle unexpected challenges, such as more than a dozen years of truce with the kingdoms around us. Don't laugh! You may think that peace is a simple thing to maintain—but without a convincing show of strength it can easily fall to pieces. I write a note to myself to write a note to Joav, my first in command, to march around the land with our military forces, putting our might on parade.

I pass by the glass displays at the far end of the court. One contains the mummified head of Goliath, the second contains an assortment of crowns that used to belong to various kings I conquered, and the third—our sacred scriptures. The fourth display contains a map, drawn with colored sand, showing all the territories belonging to my empire, and their borders, which have remained undisrupted in recent years.

I step close to it and back away from it, examine it top to bottom and side to side, all the while pleating my forehead so my scribes may note how utterly busy I am, and find someone else to bother.

All that fails to slow them down. They quicken their step to catch up to me. Then, finding themselves at close range, they jump ahead of me and behind me, left and right, shooting their questions, all of which are basically the same.

"Why, why are you so quiet about the rape?" asks one.

And the other wonders, "Is it only for now?"

So what choice do I have but pretend to be hard of hearing, which is of no use, of course, as it makes them raise their voices even louder.

"Your majesty," cries Nathan. "Shouldn't there be consequences for committing a crime?"

And Gad hurries to follow suit. "You must do something, anything really, to avenge the rape of your daughter. Not only because you're her father but also because you're the king."

"Justice must be served, your majesty," says Nathan. "If you don't act soon, the criminals hiding among us may think they have your tacit permission to do as they wish."

"The entire land may become lawless," warns Gad. "Even with no threat from outside, the empire may collapse from within."

With a heavy step I turn away from him, back to my stage.

Meanwhile Nathan repeats his original question, just to make sure it rings in my ear loud and clear. "Why, why don't you hold Amnon responsible?"

I climb up, mount the throne and slump into it, feeling choked. I ask you, how can I explain that, when I do not understand it myself?

In my notes I scribble the words, as I chant them, "*I am like the deaf, who cannot hear, like the mute, who cannot speak. I have become like one who does not hear, whose mouth can offer no reply.*"

And just as I wish for some relief from talking to my scribes, some distraction, a breath of fresh air blows in. The gilded door far at the back of the courtroom is being thrown open, and a princely figure, clad in a robe that flows gracefully behind him, enters the court.

My second son, Absalom, comes directly at me. I believe he has heard the questions, as well as my response, which is always the same. Silence.

Without the customary bow he approaches the stage upon which my throne is fixed. His luscious, long hair curls around his face, bringing to mind the mane of a lion. Any moment now, he may roar. But no, he tries to be in control of himself. The words that do escape from his lips tremble, at first.

"Everyone wonders about you," he says, through clenched jaws. "What are you waiting for? You're the king, are you not?"

"Years from now," say I, "when you reach my age, you'll see for yourself that such decisions aren't as easy as they seem. I can't bring myself to punish Amnon, misguided as he is, because just like you and your sister, he's my child, too—"

"A thug, is what he is!" says the prince, bristling at me. "And don't you patronize me with your so-called wisdom. Don't tell me, '*When you reach my age.*' No need for me to wait as long as that, to see what stares me right in the face, every day, every hour of the day. The black circles under my sister's eyes. Her hurt, her disgrace, her shame!"

Knowing that words will not suffice I rise from my seat, leaving the scepter behind it. Then with open arms I step down the stage to embrace him, which is when he does the unexpected. He hops up onto it and then, gripping the carved armrests, he lowers himself, with deliberately slow movements, right into my throne.

Nathan gasps. So does Gad.

Absalom picks up the scepter, and with a tone of mockery he imitates me, drawing notes in the air as he recites my own lines. "*Do not fret,*" he chants, "*because of those who are evil, or be envious of those who do wrong, for like the grass they will soon wither, like green plants they will soon die away.*"

Nathan and Gad click their tongues in disapproval. Over that noise I say, "I know how angry you must be, son."

"Me? Angry?" Absalom laughs, and shakes his hand to dismiss what I have just said. His mane of hair shakes as well, spreading its magnificent, reddish glow over the ornamented back of my throne. I cannot help admiring how gorgeous he looks and how natural and invincible he seems to be up there.

My son is just like me, the way I used to be, only more prepared than I ever was. He seems destined to rule, more so than my firstborn, Amnon, who cares little about leadership—but no, I cannot tell him that. I cannot upset the order of things.

Clearly Absalom is amused to have staked a place at the top. So I figure, he will not give up his seat—I mean, my seat—easily.

So I tell him, "I understand if you're impatient—"

"There's not a man in the land," he says, "more patient than I! Look at me, sitting here, twiddling my thumbs idly, flipping this scepter, just like you! I'm waiting to see some action out of you, waiting for grass to wither and green plants to die away, any moment, any day now!"

"Granted," say I, "what Amnon has done is wrong—"

"It's a crime," he corrects me, in an irate tone.

"True," say I, hoping to move the conversation into legal terms, so as to avoid falling prey to emotions. "Let's set our own feelings aside, as they are may be volatile to handle."

"Let's be silent," he hisses. "For now."

"No," say I. "Let's talk! Let's consider this crime. It's a complicated matter, which I can, perhaps, illustrate to you by quoting from our laws."

At a hint from me, both scribes hurry to the glass display at the end of the court, open it, and with quivering hands extract a number of old leather scrolls. Having fumbled for the right one Nathan brings it over, unfurls it with the utmost care, and starts scanning the entire length of it.

At last Gad comes to his aid, pointing out a particular section, where some of the letters have faded already.

"Ah, here it is!" says Nathan, and he quotes, "*If in the open country a man meets a young woman who is betrothed, and seizes her and lies with her, and they are found, then the man who lay with her shall give to the father of the young woman fifty shekels of silver, and she shall be his wife, because he has violated her. He may not divorce her all his days."*

"No, no, no! Not that section," say I. "It has no bearing on this case, because the rape happened not in the open country—but in the city."

Absalom bangs the scepter against his own forehead. "That's such a horrific law," he mutters, "if I ever heard one."

Taken aback Nathan gulps for air, finding it hard, somehow, to admonish him. "You're still young," he says, "and have a lot to learn."

"Young I am," says the prince. "Even so I know more than you!"

"I'm the recorder of history," says Nathan, with great pride. "More importantly I see myself as the keeper of tradition! I'm shocked, I'm utterly appalled to hear you say such words about our holy scriptures. Horrific?" he echoes, in disbelief.

"Horrific," says Absalom. "Fifty shekels? Is that what my sister is worth? And why should the father be compensated? Was he the one raped?"

"No, but—"

"What a lousy, laughable financial arrangement! Money changing hands between two men, as if this were a purchase of some domestic animal! Where's the punishment? Where's justice?" demands Absalom. "I must have missed both of them, somehow, in all that nonsensical verbiage!"

"But, but weren't you listening?" cries Nathan. "The rapist must marry his victim—"

"I was listening," insists my son. "But I can't believe my own ears! What are you proposing? Marriage as punishment?"

"Alas," says Nathan, in an pitiful effort to crack a joke, "that may be true in some families."

"When it comes as an answer to a crime, such a punishment is nothing short of absurd! Oh, what a laugh!"

"There's nothing funny about it!"

Absalom balances my scepter upon his forefinger, as if the two ends hold the scales of justice. "You're absolutely right," he says. "This is a serious matter. Forgive me for making light of it. For now, let me be quiet."

His silence feels threatening to me.

"No," say I. "Speak your mind."

So he says, "In theory, this law—such as it is—appears to punish the rapist, but in reality, it makes sure that his victim remains there, at his mercy. She is trapped, can't you see? Trapped, for the rest of her life!"

Nathan shrugs. "Such is our custom."

Burning with anger my son rolls his eyes, and his hand shakes, losing hold of my scepter. It falls with a crashing din onto the stage.

"Take a good look at that crumbling scroll. The letters have long faded," he says. "Not that they made any sense, ever! It's time for a change. Out with the old, in with the new!"

"You may not appreciate it," says Nathan, "but it does protect the victim. I mean, how will she ever have children, when no one else would marry her, now that she is damaged, having lain with a man?"

"That man," say I, "is her brother."

And Nathan says, "Naturally, he can't marry her."

"Nor does he want to," says Absalom. "Tamar had the presence of mind to suggest that he should ask you for her hand. In reply he slapped her mouth, so she wouldn't confuse him with such ideas, and once she was silent, he violated her."

Looking for a section more appropriate for this particular crime, Nathan skips to an earlier paragraph.

"Ah! Here, this is the right section!" he says. "*If there is a betrothed virgin, and a man meets her in the city and lies with her, then you shall bring them both out to the gate of that city, and you shall stone them to death with stones, the young woman because she did not cry for help though she was in the city, and the man because he violated his neighbor's wife. So you shall purge the evil from your midst.*"

"Really? This is what you call *the right section*? It has nothing, not a thing to do with this case," says Absalom, doing his best to contain a growing rage. "First, the law offers no protection, and not as much as a mention, for a virgin girl who is *not* betrothed, which is the case with my sister."

"True," says Nathan. "No such protection exists! A girl that is not betrothed belongs to no one, really—"

"Then, is she merely a piece of discarded property, a thing that can be damaged at will if there is no owner?" argues Absalom.

Which makes Nathan scratch his beard in utter confusion. "Oh," he mumbles. "This question is something new and quite unheard of! I never thought of that."

Eager to win the argument Absalom jumps out of his seat—I mean, my seat—and paces around the thing, but then thinks twice of it and clasps the ornamented back tightly with both hands.

I make no move that may be interpreted as competing with him for the throne. He is my son, after all. For now, all that stands between us is a piece of furniture, nothing more.

Still a bit perplexed Nathan says, "Regardless of the question, '*Is she merely a piece of property,*' which I think she may well be, the victim should have screamed—"

"She should," says Absalom, "as long as she feels someone would respond to her cries. I mean, as long as there's hope. But what if the victim knows, with painful certainty, that no one would come to her rescue? My brother's servants, all of them, were right there, cowering behind the bedroom door, yet not one of them dared to confront their master, nor did they open the door for Tamar—even by a crack—that she might escape."

"Well argued," say I, surprised by his clever, eloquent reasoning. Over the months that have passed since the rape Absalom must have prepared himself. Clearly, he has studied every aspect of the case and has cross-matched it with every detail of the law, committing it all to memory.

Now he glances down at me. "If this is so well argued, then what are you waiting for? Call the thug and punish him! Do it, finish the whole thing right here and now!"

I look up at him, meeting his gaze.

"In this court," I state, "I must show fairness. Both sides can present their arguments. So in the end, a trial can result in favor of Tamar—or not."

At once Absalom blurts out, "I don't believe you. This case is clear: my sister has been violated—"

"Even so, are you willing to risk her life?"

"What? How d'you mean?"

"I mean, I would have to appoint a special judge," say I, "just so there would be no appearance of me leaning one way or the other in this trial."

"So?"

"So that judge, acting on his power, which must be separate from mine, may decide not to be lenient, simply to prove himself in the eyes of the people."

"The less lenient he is," says the prince, coldly, "the better."

My gut is turning in a sharp, painful way at the thought of acting hastily, which may result in losing my daughter and my firstborn son in one fell swoop.

With a sigh, "You don't get it, do you," I ask, not expecting an answer.

"What I get," says Absalom, "is this: the punishment must be quick and severe. If you can't bring yourself to pass your own verdict, then fine: appoint someone else, right now, right this minute!"

"If I do, that judge may adhere, quite strictly, to the letter of the law. He may pass his sentence without mercy, so as to find both Tamar and Amnon guilty."

"He can't do that, can he?"

I hope he can feel my despair as I say, "Of course he can! And so, there's a chance that both of them may be brought out to the gate of the city, and be stoned to death."

Absalom just stands there, silent, for a long time.

At last, "Don't you quote the law to me," he grumbles, "when you've broken it yourself!"

"What have I done?" I ask, feeling a sudden pang in my heart, knowing where he is headed.

My son steps off the stage and comes face to face with me, eyes blazing with madness. I brace myself, sensing that he is about to raise his hand against me.

Instead he just smiles. Then, with a measured rhythm he quotes an altogether different section of the law, which he must have learned by heart. *"If a man is found lying with the wife of another man, both of them shall die, the man who lay with the woman, and the woman. So you shall purge the evil from Israel."*

His memory puts me in awe. So does the implicit blame.

I feel torn between two sentiments: I am proud of him and at the same time, fearful.

Meanwhile Nathan steps in between us. "Your father," he tells the prince, "has already paid a heavy price for his sin with Bathsheba, as God has stricken their first child dead, years ago."

"How is that a heavy price," asks Absalom, "when sins are paid for at the expense of someone else's life? Why should his child die?"

I am silent. Nathan presses on.

"Please, Absalom, let go of what happened back then. Besides," he says, "as a king, your father is above the law, so the section you quoted is ill-fitted for him—"

"I care nothing about this or that section!" cries Absalom. "Forget it, forget the law! What I want, what I must have, is one thing: justice!"

"Do you?" says Nathan. "You sure it's not vengeance you seek?"

My son grinds his teeth. If not for the distance between us and the height of the stage, I would hug him. I would shoulder the burden of his agony.

"You tell me," I say. "How should I punish Amnon? He is my firstborn. He stands to become the future king of Israel —"

"Does he deserve to be?"

"Do you?"

At that, a mad glint appears in his eye. In a blink he releases his hold from the back of the throne.

"What kind of an example would a king such as Amnon set for others?" he demands. "When he ascends to the throne, should every father in the land hide his daughters away—or, failing that, accept their fate to be raped?"

I sigh. "For now, Amnon is not in a position of power, and neither are you. There's time, plenty of time for me to consider everything you've said. Which I'll do in due course, I promise, as surely as I am the king."

At last, with a gesture that invites me to reclaim my seat upon the throne, he hops off the stage.

And as he walks backwards, facing me, feigning respect, I ask myself, "Do I deserve to be respected? What kind of an example do I set for others?"

Justice

Chapter 5

To this day, nearly two years after the rape, I am still at a loss to come up with the perfect way to respond to it. I still hesitate, despite fearing that if I do not act, someone else will.

From time to time I read my earlier notes. This one I find particularly telling of my mood, and I chant it to myself.

I said, I will watch my ways, and keep my tongue from sin.

I will put a muzzle on my mouth, while in the presence of the wicked.

So I remained utterly silent, not even saying anything good.

But my anguish increased. My heart grew hot within me.

According to my scribes there can be no other punishment for Amnon other than stoning—but even they are saying it now only in a whisper, because they know I cannot bring myself to take his life, and because they foresee the future, and the dangers it may bring.

A day will come when they will have to report to him, and rewrite the books using his version of history, no matter how corrupted he may wish it to be. He may even insist that they exaggerate how many girls he has deflowered, because in his mind it makes him more of a man.

*

Leaning over my chamber window to watch the sun rising I think I spot something new: a silhouette standing there, at the edge of the royal garden, where it falls into a deep ravine. Sunlight glows all around her. To see her more clearly I must squint.

There she stands, facing away from me: a dark figure with a slender, long shadow fluttering over the field of flowers behind her. She reminds me of my daughter and of her self-imposed absence from my home. No longer does she consider it safe.

Raising a thin arm, the figure waves a hand and releases something into the wind. It flaps once or twice between the ground-sweeping branches of the weeping willows. Then it flies higher, hovering for awhile, till at last it soars away.

I follow it as it glides this way and that in the direction of a distant oak tree, on the other side of the ravine. Caught up there, at the tip of the highest limb, the thing flickers, its folds steaming in the air like the feathers of a wounded dove.

Hours later, when the diplomats, advisors, generals, suppliers, architects, carpenters, contractors, lawyers, tax collectors and brick layers have all retired for the day, I find myself free to ride out there, beyond the edge the royal garden. On my way there, a magical mist hangs all around me, like tears, suspended.

It must have rained earlier that day, because the soil is soft. It gives way under the hooves of my stallion. Sloshing around that oak tree I come to realize what it is, hanging down from its highest branch: a shred of Tamar's garment, her coat of many colors. The fabric is aglow in the evening sun, releasing every reflection, every hue of the rainbow, up to the border of a large, irregular stain of browned blood.

*

Gripped by a mood for which I can find no words I ride back to the palace and summon my firstborn son to come before me at once, for a long overdue conversation.

Hair unkempt Amnon arrives at the court. He is wearing a crumpled shirt that slips off one shoulder and stinks of stale beer.

"I'm sleepy," he complains to me, in a lazy drawl. "Must we talk now? Can't whatever it is wait for some other time, whenever?"

"No," say I. "It can't."

And he says, "Oh well, too bad."

And I say, "Listen, son—"

"No, you listen," he dares cut me off. "Last night I tried my hand at something new!"

"What," say I, "asking forgiveness?"

"*Forgiveness*?" he repeats, as if this word is not only unfamiliar to him but also altogether unnecessary in human discourse. "What for?"

And before I have a chance to respond he goes on to say, slurring his words, "You, you'll be real proud of me, father. I tried my hand at something different, something I thought only you can do: writing poetry! Want to hear?"

"No," say I. "Not now—"

Waving his hand around with a grand, swinging gesture, and ignoring my refusal to listen, "The moon," he recites, "turns over metal roofs. It sinks in the mud, under the hooves. My whip flips, flops, and flies. The earth sighs. It offers itself, naked under the eyes of the stars. It opens its wounds, its weakness, its scars, like a woman lying, refusing me. Here in the scum, limbs spread apart for all to see, for me to come—"

"Enough!" I bellow. "Keep the dirt to yourself."

"You hate it?"

"I do."

Amnon marches around me as if he has scored a victory, somehow. "It moved you, then! So," he says, "it's poetry."

"It moved me to cover my ears," say I. "Foul language is the last thing I want to hear out of you."

Perhaps he has expected applause, or a word of encouragement for his performance, which I cannot bring myself to give.

"You're not the only one to hold a quill," he says, with an indignant tone. "Not the only one to search for inspiration—"

"What you should be searching for," say I, "is something entirely different: redemption."

At the sound of the word Amnon yawns. "What, that again? I'm too tired for thinking about such words. They're too damn big for me. Going back to bed now, if you don't mind."

"Oh, but I do!" I stamp my foot.

Which seems to surprise him. "Do you?"

"Redemption may be a big word, but I choose it now, because it fits the hour. Right now," I say, "you stand in the way of something that can barely be stopped. Don't you get it? A great punishment is coming your way! Before it finds you, you must face it—"

"You don't expect me to slay a giant, do you?" he says, undermining me by aiming a wink at my servants. To him, my past is ancient history, no more than an overblown old folk tale.

To me, it is utterly real, as if it happened yesterday. My ears can still hear the earth cracking underfoot when the Philistine collapsed, with my pebble lodged right there, in the center his forehead. I recall yanking his heavy sword, and shoving the point of it into the center of the cut neck, impaling it. My muscles still carry the memory of an unusual strain as I held my trophy, lifting it upright in my blood stained hands, to scare away the enemy.

Amnon winks again, which enrages me, in a flash, into dragging him by the ear, all the way to the opposite side of the court, to the central glass display, where the head of Goliath, preserved by Egyptian experts, is encased.

Its eyebrows are bushier than I remember, and so is the serpentine hair twisting upon itself. It seems to be hissing, creeping towards us, pressing against the glass as if to burst it open, which makes me wonder if there is still a remnant of life inside this scalp. I have to remind myself that nearly three decades have passes since the day I killed him.

Meanwhile Amnon cannot help but shudder, perhaps because of the darkness crawling out of those empty eye sockets, and even more than that, because he can see his own reflection right there, in between the huge jaws, over the sheet of glass that separates him from that thing, that memento of my earliest battle.

I let go of his ear, not before breathing into it, "Ever think of death?"

Amnon says nothing.. Instead, he gulps for air.

"We have laws," I say, pointing at the leather scrolls in the next glass display. "They spell out, with precise detail, the punishment for rape. You know what that is?"

Unable to utter a word, he shakes his head, No.

"Stoning," say I.

He shudders.

Seeing that at last I have made some impression on him I press on. "As much as I abhor such barbaric executions I can't save you, Amnon. Unless—"

"Unless what?"

"Unless you find a way to save yourself."

"How?"

I say, "How about asking forgiveness?"

And he echoes, "Forgiveness?"

"Yes, son. You must beg for mercy," I tell him. "And do it in earnest, in the most formal, public manner, falling to your knees before your sister, Tamar, in the presence of the entire family. Her brother, Absalom, must be present. So must her mother, my wife Maachah, and her grandfather, Talmai king of Geshur. The entire court must be in attendance, including your servants."

Amnon does not say No, which gives me a sliver of hope that he may do what I ask of him.

"There is a precedence," I tell him, even though I doubt he has any interest in matters of the law.

"What's that?"

"During a crucial battle my predecessor, king Saul, announced before his army, 'Cursed be any man who eats food before evening comes.' Meanwhile his son, Jonathan, came by a honeycomb in the forrest, and he tasted some of the honey, not knowing about his father's decree. For that, Saul intended to put him to death, but all his soldiers protested this verdict, as Jonathan was well loved by all. And so, Saul had to pardon his son."

Amnon listens in silence, so I go on to plead, "Son, do what I ask of you. Perhaps then, others may appeal to me to spare you from what's coming your way."

He steps away from the head of Goliath, and from me, at which time I hear a clap of hands behind us. There stands my second son, Absalom, with a little smile on his lips, which I find so beguiling.

"I'm here," he says, smiling at both of us, "to invite you."

To which my firstborn says, "Invite me? Really?"

And Absalom confirms, "Really! This is something I've been thinking about for quite a long time."

"Is it a party? A big one?" asks Amnon, and I detect a hint of caution under his glee.

"The biggest you've ever seen," Absalom says, in a reassuring tone.

I inquire, "What's the occasion?"

In reply Absalom bows low, perhaps too low, scraping the floor before me, which prevents me from reading his face.

"Your servant," he says, "has shearers come to shear my sheep, which is to say, to remove the woolen fleece. The cold winter is over, and the sheep no longer need the protection of their coats."

"I know all about that," says Amnon. "We are, both of us, sons of a shepherd."

And Absalom concurs. "Yes," he says, bowing a second time. "That we are. Will you come?"

To which Amnon says, "Sure, why not!"

Absalom leaps with excitement, which makes his luxurious hair bounce over his shoulders. Fascinated by the glow of it Amnon raises hand to touch one of his curls, which is when I note a strange thing. By instinct Absalom recoils.

"Don't you dare touch me," he blurts out. "Don't touch my hair."

Then, glancing at his own reflection in the glass and finding pleasure in it, he rearranges his curls. "We're going to have such fun," he promises his brother. "Come early. I'll be waiting for you."

To which Amnon says, "I shall."

I can already sense that because of this invitation, he has regained confidence in his brother, and will surely neglect to do what I have asked of him, thinking it unnecessary.

He will forget to beg for mercy.

"Is this an honest invitation?" I wonder, out loud. "I warn you, Absalom, don't pull wool over my eyes."

Absalom laughs. His smile seems crooked.

"Me? Never!" he promises. "You know better than anyone: shearing is an annual event, and it calls for a feast!"

"Where will it take place?"

"At Baal Hazor, which is a site near the border of the tribe of Ephraim," he says. "Will the king, and all the king's sons, and all his attendants please join me?"

Somehow the whole thing sounds too good to be true—but I accept the idea of a bond, a renewed bond between my children, because true is what I want it to be.

There is nothing more tempting than hope. I am intoxicated by it. The unity in my family must be restored. For its sake I am willing to give away reason. I am willing to risk anything, even being deceived.

Even so, just to be on the safe side, "No, my son," I say. "All of us should not go. We would only be a burden to you."

"No burden whatsoever," says Absalom, dancing around me. "I'll be ever so happy to host you, your majesty. But perhaps you're too busy to come, which I can certainly understand. In that case, just give me your blessing. It would mean so much to your servant."

"My blessing is yours, son," I tell him in a joyful voice, but my heart, for some reason, is heavy. "Remember, when the party starts I'll be thinking of you."

At that Absalom bows before me one last time, even lower than before. "If you can't come," he says, "please let my brother Amnon join us?"

Reluctant to do so I ask him, "Why should he go with you?"

Absalom gives me no good reason, except to say, in his irresistible manner, "Please, father. Just let him go."

I peer into his eyes, and ask, "Is this all about good cheer and welcome?"

"It is," he says, glancing sideways at his brother. "The sheep must be shorn."

79

And so, against my better judgement, I relent. Torn between suspicion and faith I watch the two of them, my firstborn and my second son, shake hands.

Absalom turns his head to me, brushes his fingers carefully to smooth his hair, and mentions in passing, "Last night I learned one of your psalms by heart."

"Really?" I say, greatly flattered.

As they walk away, down to the exit, there is no time for me to ask him, which one of them. From afar I hear him asking his brother, "Want to hear it?"

"No," says Amnon. "Not really."

Even so Absalom leans into his ear, and over the growing distance between us I hear him chanting, "*This is the fate of those who trust in themselves, and of their followers, who approve their sayings. They are like sheep and are destined to die. Death will be their shepherd, but the upright will prevail over them in the morning.*"

I wonder why he has chosen to commit to memory such a dark passage. Yet his voice is so melodious, so resonant, that I accept his reasons—whatever they may be—and even echo the words, "*Death will be their shepherd.*"

To which he chants, "*Their forms will decay in the grave, far from their princely mansions.*"

Then, swept into singing, "*Far from their princely mansions,*" my sons leave the court, together.

*

The sight of them smiling, matching step with one another, leaves a powerful impression in me. It brings back to me a moment I have nearly forgotten, from a time gone by, when I first came to the Valley of Ellah to bring food to Eliab, my oldest brother. He and the rest of my brothers were stationed with Saul's army, bracing themselves before the upcoming battle with the Philistines, which according to everyone around me was bound to end in defeat.

I remember how Eliab kept insisting that I should go home. He claimed I was too young, too naive to witness the spilling of blood. There was a sense of fear in the air—but in spite of that I was stubborn enough not to obey him, simply because.

Given the poor provisions, he was famished. I untied my satchel from the saddle, lifted the flap, removed my lyre from the top so he could take a good look inside. "Here," I said, "take a sniff."

My brother seemed to swoon at the sight of food, and at once his eyes teared up. It must have been more than a simple hunger. I believed then, and I still believe to this day, that he was overcome by a memory of home.

He must have imagined the steam, the way it would puff up the dough, just before cooling down to create the air pocket in the center of the bread. He must have conjured the touch, the soft touch of my mother's hand as she would sprinkle sesame seeds all over the top.

Eliab grabbed the satchel from my hand. I snatched it right back. But despite our game—despite all that push and pull—there was one thing that wrapped over us: the warmth of our kitchen, back home in Bethlehem.

I snap out of my memories, noting that lately I tend to spend too much time in them. My boys are gone, and the echoes of their steps have vanished.

I look around me at the decor of my palace, in which I have invested so much time and thought, not to mention gold and silver. At last, the renovation is complete. The workers have packed away their tools, stored away the ladders, removed the scaffolding, and left. In their absence you can now see the entire space, and take in its magnificence.

New, exotic draperies are hanging from the gilded trim above the arched windows. Their fringes are delicately embroidered in silver, and threaded with fine gems. The entire floor has an abstract geometrical design done in mosaic, with colored stones and marble. The walls are covered by cedar wood panels with fancy inlays in them, contrasting various stains and directions of wood grain. Flames are flickering in glass oil cups in the large metal chandeliers, which makes the vast space sparkle with light.

This is so different from my humble home, back in Bethlehem. I have created something about which I have been dreaming since the days of my youth: a grand shell for justice, learning, and power.

And like a shell, it is fragile.

I pray that my boys would create their own memories of this place, because if not for brotherhood, the rivalry between them may become deadly.

The Feast

Chapter 6

All night long, my thoughts trouble me. I am distraught over giving my permission to my firstborn son, Amnon, to attend Absalom's feast. Why? Because the sudden friendship between the two of them is simply too sudden. I mean, it takes time to build a bond. This is especially true in this case, where trust has been breached in such a blunt, terrible way, with Tamar's rape.

I go out to the royal gardens, where a cold wind whips the slender palm tree, bending its solitary shoot till its crown of leaves shakes, rattling violently as if it were about to slip down. There I hunker down, listen to the wild beat of my heart, and wait. I wait for the night to end, hoping that by sunrise I may find some relief, some deliverance.

The storm sings, yet I am silent. But after a while, listening to its rhythm, I match it with words, I intone, *"My heart is in anguish within me. The terrors of death have fallen on me. Fear and trembling have beset me, horror has overwhelmed me. I said, 'Oh, that I had the wings of a dove! I would fly away and be at rest.'"*

In the moonlight, silvery dust swirls around me. Blow by blow it rises before my eyes. Through its veil, the view of the mountains around Jerusalem is truly magical. It makes me ache to find my way back to the caves and crevices where I used to dwell. Perhaps because of my folly— the folly of a man who has known success and tired of it—I yearn for way things were, long before I became king.

These were times of danger, as Saul put his dogs on my scent. Life was thrilling. I thrived on risk.

Not so now.

I am beside myself with fear, which I cannot even explain to myself. Forget the palace. Forget the crown. It's no good, being me, being where I am.

As if listening to a stranger I hear my voice, chanting, "*I would flee far away, and stay in the desert. I would hurry to my place of shelter, far from the tempest and storm.*"

When at long last morning comes I instruct my servants to meet me in the courtyard, to rebuild the scaffolding that was left over from the recent round of renovation, the same way only higher. I must have a commanding view of the road leading up to the palace. I must be the first to spot any messengers, and to hear the news arriving from Baal Hazor, which is where Absalom would be holding his sheep sheering feast.

"Here, your majesty," says one servant. "I've built a platform upon the scaffolding, and fastened it for you, as secure as can be."

"And I," says a second one, who stands on his shoulders, "lifted your throne into place."

"For you," says the first, "I've built three stairs leading up to the it. They may look a bit too narrow, and a bit too high as well, much like a ladder—but trust me, you'll be perfectly safe."

Then, having driven the final nail, and having spread a long, beautifully woven rug at my feet, they position themselves as my guards. The heels of their boots ping against the cobblestones left and right of me as we advance. The stairs are unusually high, so I must balance myself using my scepter as I climb to the top, on my way to the throne. The third stair creaks under me, and so does the platform up there, at the top. The sound may be amplified by the void underneath, but no matter.

There I sit, gazing into the distant haze, waiting.

*

After a while my two guards nod off, which I know, because they are standing utterly still. I listen to distant sounds. I wait. I watch.

In the distance, gnarled shadows of olive trees on one side of the road are crossing it, pointing west. By noon they shrink into minute stubs, only to be chased away in the other direction, by shadows twisting east, cast by olive trees on the opposite side. Now, streaks of darkness are lengthening across the entire landscape.

It is night.

And just as I am allowing myself to breathe with some relief, because the lack of news gives me hope, I see a light strobing down the road, between one silhouette of olive tree and the next one, and the one after that, as the flame of a torch flies forth, coming towards me. I begin to hear the footsteps of a runner, thumping closer. Then, in dread, I hear his crazed voice.

"Murder!" he shrieks. "Murder!"

I leap to my feet, and the wooden platform makes a sighing sound under me. My throat is dry. It would not let me talk.

Somehow I manage to step down the stairs, nearly tumbling off them.

"Run!" he cries, coming nearer. "Run for your life!"

My guards stop him. They ask, "Why, what happened?"

"No one knows exactly," says the messenger, trying to catch his breath. "I hear that he, he—"

"Who?"

"Absalom, he, I hear he's struck down everyone, all the king's sons! Not one of them is left. Run!"

At the sound of his frantic screams, people start racing every which way across the courtyard, echoing him and waving their hands about in great confusion.

Meanwhile, shaken by the calamity, the loss of so many lives in my family, I tear my clothes and collapse to the ground.

One by one, all my attendants come to a stand by me as I lie there, as I curl in agony. Rip after rip, they tear their clothes.

Someone tries to help me to my feet, but I wave my hand and push him away.

"Your majesty," he pleads, "listen to me—"

"Go away," I mutter.

By his voice I know who he is, and I know not to trust this young fellow, because it was by his crooked advice that the trouble began. He is the advisor who helped Amnon figure out how to trap my daughter, Tamar, in his house, which led to her rape.

But Jonadab refuses to leave my side. Thinking, perhaps, that I am in shock, that I cannot hear him, he goes on to repeat, over and over again, "Please, my lord, listen to me, as my advice is greatly valued, all around town."

"Advice?" I grumble. "What advice do I need, now? Away with you, can't you see I'm grieving?"

"Please," he says, "listen to me. You'll thank me later."

"That I doubt."

To which he says, "I understand quite well, my lord, why you may dislike me—"

"Do you."

"Even so, my advice is sound."

"What d'you suggest I do?

"Wait."

"What for?"

"More messengers to come. Wait for them. There's still hope!"

"Hope?" I grumble. "What hope?"

"This messenger seems a bit scattered to me. He heard something, but wasn't there himself to witness what happened, so you can't rely on him to learn what it all means, now can you, my lord?"

I rise slowly to my knees, praying he is right.

My servants surround me, and help me get up. They steady me till I find my footing. Then they dust off my knees.

"Your majesty," says Jonadab, "you shouldn't think that all the princes are dead."

"I'll wait," say I. "You're right. Perhaps there's hope."

"For all of them," he says, "except Amnon. Only he is dead."

I hold myself back from gasping, and very quietly I ask, "How would you know?"

"Because," he says, "everyone could see—and you must have guessed it, too—that this has been Absalom's intention ever since the day my master, Amnon, disgraced his sister."

I hear the shiver in my voice as I say, through clenched teeth, "Absalom is not his brother's keepers—but he's not a murderer, either."

Jonadab plays up to me, in a manner that is plainly sleazy. "You have such a great mind," he says, "a trusting one!"

"My sons are my flesh and blood! Who can I trust if not them?" I ask, hearing a catch in my voice.

To which he says, "No one."

Amazing—is it not?—how desperately I cling to hope. Until the next messenger arrives I will imagine that my firstborn, Amnon, is still breathing, still alive, and that so are the rest of my sons. They are all well. They must be.

Meanwhile I wish to hear nothing more out of this oily fellow, because his mind, it seems, is bent on getting something out of me, using my moment of weakness to his advantage. Now that he believes his master, Amnon, to be dead, he is offering me free advice, trying to flatter me into employing him.

I wave him away when he grovels before me, when he insists on repeating, "My lord the king shouldn't be concerned, not at all, about the report that all the king's sons are dead. Only Amnon, and no one else, is dead."

Meanwhile a second torch comes into view. A second runner will arrive here shortly, bringing me a second version of today's news. I take a deep breath, bracing myself for it.

My sons are all well. They are alive, all of them. They must be.

*

The messenger kneels before me, and places his head and both palms on the ground, in total submission.

"Rise," I command.

Unlike the previous one he is silent. His face is grim. His lips are dry.

I tell my servants to bring him something to drink, to revive him. "Here, take a sip," I tell him.

The messenger takes a gulp, raises his eyes to me, and for a long time, he is watching me watching him.

At last I say, "Speak!"

And in a careful, measured manner of speech, he says, "I come from Absalom's feast."

"Describe it for me, in detail. I want to know exactly what happened, from the beginning."

Words start gushing out of his mouth as if a dam has burst open in him. "At the beginning," he says, "this was the most joyful, sumptuous affair I've ever seen. It was set outdoors, in full view of the shearing of the sheep. Local musicians danced along the space, which separated our table from the next one. They played merry tunes, and we were all singing along together. The sound was interrupted by nothing except a little bleat, here and there."

"Was there a big crowd?" I inquire. "How many of Absalom's friends were present?"

"Dozens of them! They huddled together, sitting along the wooden benches, chinking their cups against the surface of the table, so the servants would hurry up already and bring wine and beer."

"And the prince, Amnon? Was he sitting there, among them?"

"He was," confirms the messenger. "Amnon sat directly across from me. He was singing those shepherd songs, trying to keep up with the rest of the guests, but mangling the words from time to time, because he was unfamiliar with them. He sounded a bit out of tune, too, because by then he was already a bit tipsy."

"Did he take part in the conversation?"

"Well, from time to time he got up, and leaning over the table for support, because he must have felt unstable on his feet, he raised his cup and his voice, and shouted good wishes in honor of the host, I mean, his brother Absalom, who was not even there, at first."

"And when at last he arrived, did the two brothers shake hands? Did they embrace each other?"

"No," says the messenger. "At first Absalom was too busy down there, at the front gate, greeting the arriving guests, among whom I spotted the rest of the king's sons. He directed them to the other tables, which were already laden with a splendid assortment of breads and cheeses."

"And while he was greeting the guests, what was Amnon doing?"

"Not much. At one point I looked into his eyes, and what I saw was loneliness. He must have felt like an outsider. In spite of that, he tried to fit in."

"In what way?"

"Amnon started telling jokes and laughing even before the punchline, and patting his brother's friends, to whom he was a stranger, on their shoulders, as if he had known them for years, as if he couldn't be happier to meet them again."

"How did they take it?"

"I suppose," says the messenger, "that they felt obliged to suffer this familiarity, at least at the beginning."

"And then?"

"Then Absalom came, and took his time circling around our table. They all cheered him, except for Amnon who started shouting again, perhaps because he was anxious for his brother to notice him, and give him a nod of recognition."

"And meanwhile, was Absalom talking with anyone around the table?"

"From where I sat, he seemed to be whispering something, some secret instruction to each and every one of the guests, except for his brother. By now Amnon looked tired, and a bit moody, too. His head started lolling to one side."

"He must have been utterly drunk," say I, "to let down his defenses like that."

The messenger presses on. "And those at the table, they all exchanged glances and chuckled behind their hands, as if planning some childish prank on him."

"D'you know what Absalom told them?"

Here, the messenger slows down. "Forgive me, your majesty," he says. "I was far out of earshot. By the time the man next to me hissed the secret in my ear, I could barely hear it."

"Come now! That, I don't believe!"

"Truly, your majesty," says the messenger, in a tone of apology. "I couldn't hear him whisper, because a big commotion had erupted, and our table was knocked over, and——"

"Wait, wait, slow down," I cut in. "Before you tell me about the problem with the furniture I want to hear a bit more about that secret. What was it? You must have figured it out, by now."

"I have," says the messenger. "Forgive me, your majesty. I'm reluctant to repeat it."

"Don't be afraid," I tell him. "First, this is not your secret to keep. And second, I won't punish you for repeating it. You have my word."

He takes a long pause, after which he says to me, "Absalom ordered his men, Listen, when my brother, Amnon, is in high spirits from drinking wine and I say to you, 'Strike him down,' then kill him. Don't be afraid. Haven't I given you this order? Be strong and brave.'"

*

At this point I need not listen to him anymore. The messenger drones on, describing what he witnessed after that, and how horrible it all was, and how he fled. His voice comes to me, muffled, as I press my hands against my ears, my temples, my eyes, blocking his presence. I must ignore him, and everyone and everything around me, so as to lose myself in grief, and in despair.

This was no murder. There is no other name for it but execution.

I stare at the darkness of the palms of my hands and at once, images of that *feast*—for lack of a better term—light up in my mind. I hear every sound in that place, and take in every smell, as if I have witnessed the entire affair myself, as if I own the senses of the killer and of the victim at once, as if I am possessed by them, because they are, both of them, my own flesh and blood.

I shudder to see so many daggers drawn out of metal holsters. Their harsh grating noise penetrates me. A gasp, a last gurgle of surprise escapes from Amnon's throat, as many hands grip him, and twist his arms forcefully behind his back.

The bleating of sheep is heard faintly in the background as blades rise, flashing in the air. Then they plunge upon his throat, clinking against each other, and the first of them slashes the vein.

His bloodied corpse is thrown, like leftover meat, by the side of the bench where he has sat. Overhead, birds of prey start hovering. Flies are buzzing, buzzing all around, sensing the sweet taste of blood, which is spurting from his neck.

His eyes turn. They go on turning in their sockets, nearly flipping over in an unnatural way, as if to see the man standing directly behind him. Absalom. There, there he is, striking a victorious pose: legs wide apart, arms crossed, giving him what he has wanted: a nod, a final nod of recognition.

Oh, my son, Absalom.

In Hebrew it means, *Father of Peace*. What a beautiful name I gave him at birth, and how far from it he has now gone. I wonder: can this rift, between him and his name, ever be bridged?

Meanwhile the guard, who is standing watch next to the gate, calls me.

"Your majesty," he cries, "look up! I see men in the direction of Horonaim, on the side of the hill."

And at once Jonadab says to me, as if to prove a point, "See, the king's sons have come! It has happened just as your servant said."

As he finishes speaking, my younger sons come in, dismount their mules, and run to me, wailing. I, too, and all the attendants around us start weeping bitterly.

In my chamber, later that night, I find myself unable to stop thinking about Absalom. With his elder brother out of the way, he has now become two things at once: the rightful heir to the throne, and a wanted criminal.

I must think how to respond to this new, puzzling situation.

Meanwhile I bring my hands again over my eyes again, and in a snap I find myself back there, at the feast, a few hours earlier. I imagine him standing there, over the corpse, which is still warm. Behind him, the rest of my sons get up in a big haste, mount their mules, and flee. Absalom alone remains in place, setting his foot firmly over the pulled-back shoulder of the corpse.

Of all his friends, he is the only one without a dagger—yet the blood of his brother is on his hands.

In my mind I hear him say a single word: his victim's name, "Amnon." It is with dismay that he says it, because we both know what it means.

Trust.

I paint an image in my mind: Absalom shakes his magnificent, red hair so it spreads over his shoulders. He brushes through it with his long fingers. Then, with a smile that contorts his beautiful face into a strange new expression, he raises his wine goblet up high, and starts pouring it over the wounds of his brother.

I see him looking directly at me, as if there is no distance between us, as if to him my hands are transparent, and cannot mask my face, the horror in my eyes. And handing me his empty glass, he winks at me in a mock salute.

A Desolate Woman

Chapter 7

For many days, weeks, months, I mourn for my firstborn, Amnon—and not only for him but also for Absalom, knowing that to do what he did, something inside him must have snapped. He is forever changed. No longer is he the child I knew.

In a single moment I lost both my sons.

Three years have passed since that day, and my spies tell me that Absalom is now living out of my reach, in the only place he considers safe: the palace of his grandfather, Talmai king of Geshur, who is certain to protect him. Despite being my ally in every other respect, old Talmai is known for being stubborn. He will undoubtably refuse to hand him over to me.

But for now I make no such request. Why? Because if Absalom were to be brought back here, to Jerusalem, how should I deal with him? Should I throw him behind bars—or else recognize him, as some of my advisors suggest, as my heir, a man of privilege whose crime deserves nothing more than a symbolic slap on the wrist?

I am faced not only with a political problem but also a deeply personal one. By now I am consoled concerning Amnon, yet I am afraid of my own reaction at that critical moment, when I first lay eyes on the man responsible for his death.

Will I be overwhelmed by rage—or else, love? Will I hug my son, who has been long lost to me—or else, will I fly madly at him? Either way I doubt I will be able to control myself, and hide from Absalom how dearly I have longed for him.

I am a father. This role has changed me: when he was a child I may have looked strong in his eyes—but now I am vulnerable.

No one but me knows how these doubts gnaw at me. I carry on with matters of the state, and to all appearances I am a happy man. I attend plays, sheep shearing feasts, sword fights, hunting trips. I laugh at official parties. I make love to my wives. I send gifts to my daughter, Tamar, who keeps returning them back to me.

Now that her brother is a fugitive she lives alone in his house, with no one to talk to, a desolate woman.

I hear her name mentioned, from time to time, especially in conversations between two of my wives: her mother Maachah, who barely talks to anyone around the court, simply because she does not have to, as she is of royal blood, and my lovely Bathsheba, who has her way of getting the other women to trust her, and listen to her advice.

Just this morning, as I passed by the women's quarters, I caught sight of her, brushing Maachah's hair, one strand after another, in front of the mirror.

"What can I do?" asked Maachah. "My daughter, Tamar, won't talk to me. She won't talk to anyone. I have no idea what's in her heart."

"I do," said Bathsheba.

Maachah turned around in her seat. "Really?"

"Really. Your daughter has been brought up as a princess, and so have you. As such, both of you have been carefully separated—until now—from the affairs of other woman, women less fortunate than you, less powerful. I've seen them owned and disowned by men. I've seen them trapped, molested, robbed, maimed, even killed."

Maachah raised her head, half of which has already been styled with huge curls. She tilted it all the way back, so as to look at Bathsheba down her nose. And with arrogance, she sneered. "How, may I ask, did you get to see all that?"

"I used to be a soldier's wife."

"Clearly," said Maachah, "you don't belong here, in the palace."

Without taking offense, "I belong everywhere," said Bathsheba. "I am every woman out there, because I know what it means to be violated."

Maachah blurted, in an acid tone, "I bet you do."

"And so," said Bathsheba, "I know how your daughter must be feeling right now."

At that Maachah took a long pause.

At last, "You think she blames me?" she asked, this time in a meeker tone.

To which Bathsheba replied, "No! You shouldn't think that way."

"How about David? You think she blames him?"

"No. She's a gentle soul, and the only one she blames is herself, for allowing herself to be trapped."

"You sure?"

"I am. A raped woman is considered damaged goods around here. Knowing it Tamar feels ashamed. Guilty, even. Which is why she is still trapped in her own mind. She can't find a way to forgive herself."

"But she must move on, somehow," whispered Maachah. "It's been three years."

"Yes," said Bathsheba. "Three years, during which you haven't talked to her, not really."

"I don't know how."

"Please forgive me for saying so: I feel for you, I do."

Maachah wiped the corner of her eye. For a while she said nothing, perhaps fearing that if she would, she might start sobbing and never stop.

At last she whispered, "You're right. I've lost her." Then, "Talk to her," she begged, suddenly reduced to tears. "Do it for her, for both of us."

Bathsheba smiled. She turned Maachah around to face the mirror. Then, in a long, smooth motion, she started brushing the next strand of her hair, after which she curled it and fixed it with a golden thread to the top of her head.

Maachah clasped her hand. "Guide us. Bring Tamar back to me, will you?"

"Don't you worry," said Bathsheba. "I will."

*

It is the end of the day, and light in my chamber has dimmed. I go out to the roof. and set the torch, leaning out of its corner, aflame. At once, shadows start spinning around it as I move to the other corner.

I take a peek through the lattice, here along the edge, searching for the last glint of sun. What I find is nothing but a scattered haze, a darkness within and without.

Then I sense arms wrapping around me, and a dear, familiar scent.

"David," she breathes in my ear, "I have a favor to ask of you."

To which I say, "Anything."

Turning to face her I see that her eyes are clouded with worry, so I decide to be as magnanimous as I can, simply because such is my pleasure.

"What's troubling you, Bathsheba, and what is your request? Be it as much as half the kingdom I shall give it to you!"

Raising an eyebrow, "Really," she says, decidedly unimpressed. "You know, I *could* say yes to that."

"Really?" say I, taking a cautious step back, because suddenly I figure that half the kingdom is a whole lot, and a whole lot is not all that easy to give away. "I must be more careful with my words. Sometimes I get swept away by them."

"And I thought," she says, playfully now, "that what sweeps you away is love."

"Oh yes, that too."

Again, her face turns serious.

"I'm here," she says, "because of words. Your words."

Hoping that for once she is willing to pay me a compliment for them I say, "So glad to hear it! My words are truly the best of me. They're something in which I take great pride."

To which she smiles. "I know you do."

With the rest of my wives I am smitten by their wonderfully accurate praise—or so it seems to me—of my literary work. Yet part of me suspects that quite a few of them never read a word of it, and others have yet to develop the skill of understanding what they read. But when it comes to Bathsheba I am smitten by who she is, in spite of the fact that she chooses never to flatter me.

But tonight, things may be different.

I find myself feeling like a boy, which often happens to me in her presence. "I can't even describe how much I would value even a single word of encouragement, especially when it comes from you," I say, excitedly. "It'll make our love even more perfect than it already is."

Meanwhile Bathsheba turns sideways, which reveals to me that the elegant dress she is wearing is backless, that the silk swooshes with each sway, each step, and that there is a long slit in it, starting at the neckline, which hints at her cleavage. Out of it she pulls an fine, embroidered purse, and out of that, a scroll.

"Here," she says. "This is the last piece of yours I've read. Look, is this your handwriting—"

"What, what's this?" say I, gasping now, because this scroll looks utterly familiar. It is not the type I use for my psalms, as it is made of leather, not papyrus. I take the thing, with great care, from her fingers, and pull it open.

She says, "It's what you wrote, three years ago, having learned what happened to your daughter, Tamar."

I hang my head between my shoulders. For a long while I remain silent.

In a severe tone, "This," I say at last, "is not for anyone to read."

"Not even me?"

"Not anyone."

"That's what I thought," says she. "And that's exactly what I want to discuss with you."

To which I say, "There's nothing to discuss. It's my mistake: I should've burned this thing."

"No," she says, daringly. "You shouldn't."

I know my face is turning red because it feels hot, and because she glances at me with astonishment.

"Woman, are there no bounds to curiosity?" I mutter. "You must have known that I hid this scroll from view."

"Was it wrong of me to talk to you about it?"

"Talking about it is the least offense of all! It was wrong of you to unearth that which I buried, that which I wanted to forget. It was wrong of you to unfurl the thing, to read it, to take it. Wrong, wrong, wrong!"

Bathsheba looks up into my eyes in that endearing manner of hers. "How can you blame me?"

To which I say, "How can I not?"

"Curiosity is in my nature, and from time to time it forces me to do things which you, being so much more informed than me, may deem silly, or even downright dangerous. Please," she says, in her soft, velvety tone, "don't hate me for it."

Refusing to be disarmed so easily by her charms I roll my eyes. I am angry at her, and even more so at myself. "If you could get your hands on it, so can my scribes. Now, armed with what I've written about the matter, they may report it—"

"I hope they do," she says.

"No!" I cry. "Trying to control the way they do it is going to be a nightmare for me, and it would force me to think of that terrible day, and that rape, all over again."

She starts caressing my shoulder, my arm, my wrist, getting closer and closer to the scroll. "I shouldn't have taken it without your permission," she says. "For that, David, forgive me."

I raise my hand up to the torch that leans over our heads. A sudden gust of wind whips the flame into roaring. Then the tongue of fire licks the curled edge of the leather, as if yearning to sate its hunger.

"I'll burn the thing," I say, "right now!"

She snatches the scroll away from me, and hides it behind her back. "You will do no such thing! This is a crucial piece of writing, the closest you ever got to describing something meaningful to me, something truly important!"

Leaning this way and that around her I try to grab the scroll back, in vain.

"As writing goes I neglected, in my haste, to polish it," I tell her. "I can't believe you find this of any value. It has none of my signature style—"

"What it has," she says, "is truth."

"No one may even recognize it as mine. It's too raw."

"Which is why it's so poignant!"

Only now do I notice that she is touched, deeply touched by it, to the point of praising my writing—but in spite of having waited years for that to happen I am too focused at the moment on reaching around her, and releasing that scroll from her hold.

By now Bathsheba has slipped away from me. There she is, at the other corner of the roof. So what choice do I have but to chase her?

I come. She goes. At every turn I find myself blocked, because the pots of fragrant roses, which are set at measured intervals along the wooden lattice, are always in the way between us. If I am to the right of them, she is to the left, and if she is to the right, I am to the left. Round and round we go, my royal robe fluttering behind me, her silk dress flowing in the breeze.

I come. She goes. This corner. That corner. To and fro and back again. When at last she lets me catch up to her I bend over my knees, panting.

Drawing closer to me, she tucks the scroll in the safest place: her cleavage. Then she murmurs, "Oh David," and again, "you're so irresistibly handsome, even now."

At that I straighten my back at once, waiting to hear more sweet nothings from her. She sets her little foot on top of mine, rises to her tiptoe, and wraps her arms around my shoulders, which makes me feel big, and as invincible as I used to imagine I was, back in my youth.

I open the flaps of my royal robe and bring her in, to protect her from the chill. I hug her to my chest, and lose myself in her touch. She kisses me, and her lips are so sweet, so soft against my hardness.

The night swirls around us. We cling together. We are one.

Brushing my lips against her forehead I feel that she has pleated it just now. It is written with worry.

Noting that I am trying to read her, she asks me, "Why?"

And I echo, "Why what?"

She brings out the scroll, puts it in my hands, and covers it, ever so tenderly, with hers. "Why on earth d'you wish to destroy it?"

"Because."

"Because what?"

"Isn't it obvious?"

"If it were, would I be asking?"

I sigh. "No one should learn the sordid facts of that horrible thing, that assault."

"Why shouldn't they?"

"Because," say I. "That would be like violating my daughter all over again."

"About that," says Bathsheba, "you're quite mistaken."

"Am I?"

"Yes," she says. "You are. In your mind, history belongs to the victor. Triumphs should be glorified, failures—glossed over."

"But of course! That's the way it's always been."

"It's been that way, perhaps too long."

"What d'you mean, *perhaps too long*?"

"I mean, the way it's always been isn't necessarily the right way."

"What other way is there?" I ask, and without waiting for an answer I press on, with great ardor. "Every day I dedicate myself, with everything I have in me, to one project: committing my story—or at least, the better parts of it—to the books, for the sake of the House of David, for the sake of my descendants and the entire nation. My version of events, setting up a model of a shining hero, will live on, in our times and for posterity."

"For what purpose?"

"To excite the mind for greatness."

"A valiant effort," she says. "You are a victor among victors, and without a doubt, yours is a story to be remembered, in *all* its parts. But why not allow the victim her voice?"

"By which you mean what?"

"Look, if history belongs to the victor, it follows that cruelty is lionized, and that the names of villains, murderers, robbers, and rapists are hailed, in war and peace alike, at the expense of silencing the names of the conquered."

"I get it, I do."

"Do you, really?"

"Yes," I say. "With a little less luck, my name could've been stricken off the books, or mentioned in passing as a traitor. If Saul had it his way I could've remained a nobody."

"I'm glad you see it my way," says Bathsheba. "Singing the praises of the victors is fine—but then, if that's all we hear, who will speak for the downtrodden?"

She has a point, which is why I must argue against it. I close my hand upon the scroll, and shake my fist in the air. "History admires those who are strong! It is this that makes me strive to achieve great things."

Bathsheba gives me a look.

"If history ignores those who are weak," she says. "then the name of your daughter will be lost."

"It'll be hidden," say I, "to protect her."

"Her suffering will be obliterated, and so will her identity. It'll be as if she never existed."

"Given what she's gone through, it's for her own good."

"Is it?"

I hesitate to answer, because she makes me doubt that which I have held true all my life. I hate it when that happen.

With an amused smile at me Bathsheba says, "I can just imagine your scribe, Nathan, chewing the tip of his quill, so he may spit out something lyrical yet benign about your daughter, something that will obscure who she really is, and how bravely she tried to overturn her fate."

"I can see him in my mind," say I. "I can just hear him mumbling, under his beard, as he scribbles something like, '*Now that her brother is a fugitive she lives alone in his house, with no one to talk to, a desolate woman.*'"

"Give her a voice," says Bathsheba, in a tone that is intense, and full of pity for Tamar, and for all of us. "Let everyone hear how a woman does all she can, with such amazing courage, to resist a rape. Let her story be told!"

"That," say I, "will take a change in the way things are."

Her eyes shine. "Yes," she says. "A tremendous change! Up to now you managed to see to it that your scribes would gag their own mouths, to avoid mentioning the names of some of the women in your life."

"The history they write," say I, "is the history of men."

"Don't I know it," says Bathsheba. "All Nathan wrote about me is the fact that I was bathing one night. It tickled his imagination, I suppose—but of what value is it? There is more to me than that, don't you think?"

I must admit, "A whole lot more."

"But never mind me," she says. "It's different with Tamar. She's your daughter, and more eloquent than any one of your sons."

"About that, you're absolutely right."

"Do me this favor, David—"

"For you, anything!"

"Let her voice be heard," she says, eagerly, "for the sake of all women!"

I cannot resist Bathsheba when she speaks with such passion —but what I can do is let her work a bit harder to get what she wants. So I strike the pose of a thinking man.

"Let Tamar speak through your words," she begs, "because it is from her that you took them! Or else, she will forever stay mute. Forever will she remain a desolate woman!"

I say nothing, for just a bit longer.

Which brings her close to tears. "Let the silence end!"

Then she adds, "Give me that scroll, as well as your permission to hand it over to your scribe, Nathan, that he may record it in the scriptures. If you do, one day Tamar may come back here, and thank you for it."

And on this note, unable to resist her any longer, I give in. History belongs to both men and women, so in the most profound sense, what Bathsheba is asking for is half the kingdom.

She deserves it. I must yield.

I open the palm of my hand and let her take the story from me, to do with it what I know is right.

A moment later Bathsheba is gone.

And for several weeks after our conversation I sense a change, a new calm in me, perhaps because now I anticipate seeing my daughter again. I trust she will be back in my arms—not immediately, but perhaps one of these days.

Every morning, looking out of my chamber window, I see the old oak tree, bent there over the edge of the deep ravine. It reminds me of myself.

Every evening I ride out there, and raise my eyes to the highest branch, the one that has lost nearly all its leaves. At the tip of it still hangs the shred of cloth, the last remnant of Tamar's beautiful coat. Its many colors are streaming wave after wave in the breeze, obscuring what I know must still be there: a stain of blood. I lean against the trunk. I listen to the sound of the frayed thing. It is rustling overhead, whispering promise, forgiveness, hope.

To every thing there is a season, and a time to every purpose under the heaven.

I close my eyes and new psalms come to me, which I commit to memory so that I may write them in my scroll, later that night. Thinking of Tamar I hum softly, I sing, *"In embroidered garments she is led to the king. Her virgin companions follow her, those brought to be with her. Led in with joy and gladness, they enter the palace of the king. Your sons will take the place of your fathers. You will make them princes throughout the land."*

I draw long, slanted letters in my mind, and ask myself, Who will run their eye through my writing? Who will be swept by this ache I feel, this longing for my long lost girl?

In reply, my mind takes a new spin. It invents my readers out of thin air. Seeking a secluded place, two lovers will come here one day in the distant future, sometime in the years, decades, and centuries after my body has long crumbled into dust.

Here they will spread a blanket upon the earth, and reclining upon it they will take in the smell of fallen leaves, and listen to the dry crinkle, and to the chirping of birds returning here, to their wintering grounds, as even the stork in the heavens knows its seasons.

Then the two lovers will unfurl my scroll together. They will take turns reading it to each other, filling in some of the words where the ink has faded.

When that autumn comes I will be here, present but obscure, like dust, blanketed. I will hear their voices, breathing life into my poetry, endowing it with their own spirit, their love.

Mercy

Chapter 8

A long time ago, my scribe, Nathan, fooled me into passing a verdict upon myself. I will never forget it: he did it in a roundabout way, by telling me a fable, a made-up story about some poor man's sheep, which was really a different way of looking at my sin: robbing my soldier Uriah of his wife, my Bathsheba.

I hate being fooled. Can you blame me? It is such a humbling experience. Being judged is no fun either, especially when at first I thought myself wise, just, and powerful for rebuking a sinner, only to realize that this sinner is no other than me.

Since then—as a measure of caution—I avoided passing judgement on others. Instead I delegated that responsibility to assigned judges, which created a judicial hierarchy under me. But recently, perhaps out of boredom, I have started to attend some of the trials and legal appeals. For me, they present matters of law that challenge the mind. More importantly, they distract me from my own worries.

Meanwhile my first in command, Joav, son of my sister Zeruriah, seems to have despaired of the opportunity for war, as all is boringly quiet on all fronts. No longer does he suggest that I define this or that king as an enemy of the empire. Instead he keeps urging me—for no apparent reason—to be more involved in judicial proceedings, and even go back to presiding over them.

He twists his mustache between his fingers, sharpening its tip. "No one's sense of justice comes close to yours," he says.

"Really?"

"Really, your majesty."

Years ago, my nephew was the first one to address me as *your majesty*, which was nothing but flattery, of course. I found the sound of it pleasant, even though the title was undeserved, because at the time I was a fugitive, and according to common wisdom, had no future ahead of me.

Whenever Joav addresses me this way I have to remind myself that these words, nice as the may be, are coming from the mouth of one of the most ruthless men in the land, a killer who cares little about the law, and whose knives may have rusted a bit over the years—yet they remain dangerous even when dull, and may cause more torment than the sharpest edge.

What I find strange is why he cares what I do, especially now, in peacetime.

So I ask, "Why d'you care what I do?"

And he says, "Why shouldn't I?"

I wave my hand at him, in the manner of dismissal. "Enough," I say. "Just focus on your task, is all."

Which he resists. "Ha! My task is to fight," he says, "and lately—I mean, for the last dozen years or so—you've given me nothing, no wars, no battles, not even a minor skirmish to lighten things up for me. All you do is ponder vague things, such as the meaning of life, and such."

"So?" I shrug. "Why shouldn't I?"

"Because," says Joav. "Trust me: there is none! All these thoughts in your head, they prevent you from action, which is why you haven't decided, to this day, to bring your son back—even though everyone who has eyes in his head can see, clear and simple, that you're dying to do it."

That I ignore, so he presses on. "I'm family, which is why you should make an effort, as hard as that may be for you, and listen to me."

I pretend not to hear a word he says.

"I see," he mutters. "You're much too tender, too sensitive to even respond to me regarding Absalom."

My silence becomes really tense.

"Relax," says Joav. "I'll say nothing more about that."

To which I say, "How about you say nothing more, period?"

And he replies, over my objection, "How about just one more thing: normally, family matters are private—"

"Private," say I, cutting in, "they must remain."

Unfazed, he goes on. "In families other than ours, such matters may be a matter of gossip for the neighbors—but in no way do they affect their lives in any real, substantial way. Yet when assault, incest, and murder occur in the king's family, they affect matters of the state."

I know he is right. The rape of my daughter, Tamar, came at a significant cost, not only of her pain and of my regrets and confusion but also at the cost of having to cancel visits of many princes, who were planning to come from near and far to gaze at her beauty. During such visits many political alliances could have been forged. History would have turned out differently.

And as for the murder of my firstborn, Amnon, it has upset the prospects of a peaceful transition of power, because now, who will take my place when I am gone? Whom shall I name as my heir? God knows.

"I know that you know I'm right," says Joav. "Your majesty, you can't make believe that these crimes, committed by your children, are private. You must bring such matters to a quick resolution, and you must do it in public, which so far you were loath to do."

"I'm going to say nothing, not a word about what Absalom has done, because what I say has consequences."

"When you say nothing, your majesty, that has consequences, too."

He may be expecting me to dismiss that as utter nonsense —but when I answer with silence, he adds, "Your actions are a model for the entire nation. When you take time to make up your mind, when you show the slightest hint of hesitation, it weakens your rule and invites threats from within and without."

When I remain quiet, he prods me again.

"Even a mistake," he says, "is better than doing nothing."

"As I've already said," I repeat, now in a fainter tone, "just focus on your task."

"Ha! How can I focus on it when you don't focus on giving me a mission?"

To which I say, "Can't you just be happy for the great prosperity, and for peace in the land? Everyone else is!"

With dismay, he says, "Everyone else isn't too bright, then!"

I give him a look, so he bares his teeth in a burst of laughter. "Nothing," he says, "sharpens the mind like a good fight."

"Nothing clouds it like spilling blood."

"Ha! Spare me the sentimental claptrap," he says. "We both know that victory is intoxicating. Don't you deny it!"

"Addictive, is what it is."

"It's something that this nation has long aspired to achieve, because during most of our history, we were the weak, the downtrodden. We suffered heavy losses in one war after another. Our men were slain, our children—sold into slavery, our women—raped."

"That's how things used to be, even on good years," say I, "Even during Saul's reign, we remained in fear of our neighbors, the Philistines. But not anymore—"

"So now, it's payback time!" cries Joav, with a flash of cruelty in his eyes. "You may think this is a power game for me, but I assure you it's more than that! I feel I must avenge the long suffering of our people."

"Just like you had to avenge the blood of your brother, Asahel, defying the orders I gave you."

"Yes, just like that," he says. "Why don't you give an order? Let our army expand the empire, north and south, from Babylon to Egypt and beyond, as far as we can push it. And then, let's get drunk, because such is the sweet taste of victory!"

"I would rather stay sober."

"In the name of glory, let me wage wars in your name!"

"Are we not strong enough by now?"

"*Enough*? Is there such a thing?"

To remind him of the words uttered by Abner, the general he stabbed to death, years ago, I ask, "Should the sword devour forever?"

Joav narrows his eyes so the steel gray glint in them is lost in a shadow. "Power," he says, "must be proven, time and again, or else people take it for granted. They become lazy, and stop preparing themselves for military threats."

I ask, "Are you paying any attention to what's going on? There are no threats to speak of."

"Not yet," he says. "Your majesty, our soldiers are restless, and so am I. What's the point of training them if they can't practice their skills on a real battlefield? We're going to die of the worst cause: boredom!"

"Boring as it may sound to you I would rather have peace."

"It has a bad influence on you," he says. "In your youth you showed no hesitation when action was necessary. Not so now."

I roll my eyes, impatient for him to go away already.

"Let me help you," he pleads, making an effort to stay cool, stay polite. "Let me take you out of your feeble state."

"My state may be feeble," say I. "But the country is strong enough to take it."

Now with an undertone of threat, he says, "How much longer do I need to tolerate a leader who does nothing but play his lyre, pluck his harp, and shilly-shally in matters that put our national security at stake?"

"Fine." I sigh. "I'll think of something for you to do."

My first in command turns to go, not before casting a sideways glance at me.

"While you're at it," he says, in his most casual manner, "think of doing something yourself."

"Such as what?"

"Such as getting more involved in judicial proceedings."

I demand, once more, "Why d'you care what I do?"

And once again, Joav says, "Why shouldn't I?"

*

Because of his constant nagging I find no way to avoid listening to this woman, who has come here all the way from Tekoa, which is a village on the Eastern slopes of the Judean hills, on the edge of the rain shadow of the higher hills to the west of them.

She is here, my servants tell me, to plead for mercy for her son. Hers, they say, is a particularly complex family matter, and no wonder: Tekoa is too dry for reliable cultivation, which often leaves its farmers without crops, and eager to lay their hands on more lands and more resources needed for survival, such as access to wells and rivers. Greed often leads to violent clashes, and brings about numerous quarrels that reverberate all the way up, to my court.

The woman falls with her face to the ground to pay me honor, so at first I cannot read her expression. All I see is a strand of silver hair, spilling out of her dark veil, which tells me something about her age.

From down there she says, "Help me, your majesty!"

I demand, "What's troubling you?"

She raises her eyes to me, dabs their inner corners once or twice with a cotton handkerchief, and adjusts the veil covering her head. Then in a dry, terse manner, almost like a summary, she says, "Listen to me! I'm a widow. My husband is dead. Your servant had two sons. They got into a fight with each other in the field, and no one was there to separate them."

At the sound of this my curiosity awakens. At once I think of my own two sons, Absalom and Amnon, and the fierce rivalry that used to consume both of them while Amnon was still alive.

I have been telling myself that this is an age-old tale, that it started long ago with envy, a deadly envy between Cain and Abel, the first brothers in the story of mankind. Such struggles happen in many families, not only mine—but knowing this does not dull the pain in my heart. As a father I am lost, utterly lost in my grief.

Her next sentence echoes my thoughts. She says, simply, "One struck the other and killed him."

"I'm so sorry," say I, "for your loss."

The widow nods briefly, in formal recognition of my expression of sympathy. Yet her eyes remain cool, oddly so. They betray absolutely no emotion. I figure that she must be a strong woman, and that in her pride, she is trying to hold herself together in my presence, so as to conceal how devastated, how crushed she is by her sorrow.

Still, a part of me doubts this explanation, because I take note of what I see, which in her case is a rather well composed demeanor. I was fooled once by Amnon into ordering my daughter into his house, and a second time by Absalom, into sending Amnon to his party. Both cases ended in disaster. Still, when it comes to people outside my immediate family, I consider myself perceptive. I am known, my servants tell me, for my skill of seeing through pretense.

But with this woman, who knows? Her face is like a mask to me. Is she playing it calm, or is she calm for real?

I give a hint to my servants to set the sconces left and right of the throne aflame, so the shine will be in her face, the better for me to read her. In a blink the woman lowers her head.

I offer my condolences, once more. "May you know no more sorrow."

She dubs her nose with her handkerchief once or twice. "Now," says the widow, "the whole clan has risen up against your servant. They say, 'Hand over the one who struck his brother down, so that we may put him to death for the life of his brother whom he killed. Then we'll get rid of the heir as well.'"

I say nothing, because talking may distract me from studying her face. The woman wipes the wrinkles around her eyes, even though they seem dry. Perhaps, having mourned her dead son, she has no more tears in her. I figure that she wants to protect him from the entire clan, whose wish to exact a penalty can also be seen as greed, because with her second son executed, the property of this family will fall directly into their hands.

The story lends itself to being interpreted this way, does it not?

Clasping her hands together, "Your majesty," she cries. "They would put out the only burning coal I have left, leaving my husband neither name nor descendant on the face of the earth."

Her words must have been carefully chosen, well ahead of time. I know they are designed specifically for me, I mean, for the poet in me. They evoke such a strong image that in a flash, it ignites the pain, down in my guts.

The light flickering in the sconces behind me leaves my face in the dark, so as to obscure my reactions from those who come before me. I find myself grateful for that, because in a blink tears well in my eyes. I am tempted to use the sleeve of my royal robe, or else pluck her handkerchief out of her hand to wipe them away.

Instead I just lean back, deeper into the shadow, which helps me, somehow, to compose myself. Reluctant to make a decision out of pure emotion I decide to delay it. Let me wait until I study her case from more angles, perhaps even call members of her clan to testify before me.

"Go home," I tell her. "I'll issue an order on your behalf."

But the woman seems to understand that a delay may not be in her favor, and with amazing persistence she presses on.

"Let my lord the king pardon me and my family," she says, "and let the king and his throne be without guilt."

To which I say, "If anyone says anything to you, bring them to me, and they won't bother you again."

Still, the widow does not stir, and with a peculiar kind of stubbornness she raises her voice and says, "Then let the king invoke the Lord his God to prevent the avenger of blood from adding to the destruction, so that my son will not be destroyed."

The image makes me quiver. As a poet I am deeply moved, once again. Unable to control my pity any longer, "As surely as the Lord lives," I vow, "not one hair of your son's head will fall to the ground."

It is then that the woman rises to her feet. But instead of leaving the court, she takes a step forward, and looking me directly in the eye she says, "Let your servant speak a word to my lord the king."

"Speak," I say.

The widow lowers the veil to her shoulders. Now I know who she is: the wise woman from Tekoa, famous for offering her advice not only to her village folk but also to other people, who come flocking to her place from around the land.

To me she says, "My story is much like your own, your majesty, and the way it unfolds is in your hands."

I refrain from saying that my control over my story, such as it is, is precisely what makes coming to a decision so unbearably difficult. My power is the thing that accentuates my weakness.

"Why then have you kept your own son in exile?" she asks, daringly now. "Why have you devised a thing like this, a model of harshness, against the people of God?"

"Because," say I, "even if I wish to forgive my son for his crime, I can't."

"Why not?"

"The father in me must obey the king that I am, in the name of justice."

"In the name of mercy," she says, "give him back his life! You have that power, and you've used it quite gracefully in my case. Have you not promised me that not one hair of my son's head will fall to the ground? When the king says this, does he not convict himself, for the king hasn't brought back his own banished son?"

"By law Absalom must be executed." I shake my head. "He better stay in exile. I don't want to be the one to send him to his death."

"Like water spilled on the ground, which cannot be recovered, so we must die," says the wise woman. "But that is not what God desires! Rather, He devises ways so that a banished person doesn't remain banished from Him. Call your son back, that he may find a way to return to your embrace."

By now I am fairly certain that her tale, much like Natan's old fable, is simply a mirror image of my own predicament. It shows truth by means of an illusion.

The woman lifts her veil and wraps it over her head. By doing so, she goes back to her earlier role, not as a wise women who offers me her advice—but as a widow seeking mine.

"And now," she says, in summary, "I've come to say this to my lord the king, because the people have made me afraid. Your servant thought, 'I'll speak to the king. Perhaps he'll grant his servant's request. Perhaps the king will agree to deliver his servant from the hands of the men who's trying to cut off both me and my son from God's inheritance.' May the word of my lord the king secure my inheritance," she says, "for my lord the king is like an angel of God in discerning good and evil. May the Lord your God be with you."

During her tediously long summary, which offers no new insight on her story, my attention starts drifting. It is then that I sense the presence of someone else in the court—or to be more precise, just outside its door. Every now and again I spot something there, something sharp peeking out from behind. Now I think I know what it is: the tip of a mustache.

Raising my voice, for the benefit of that man, lurking there, I say, "Don't keep from me the answer to what I'm going to ask you."

"Let my lord the king speak," she says.

I demand, "Why would someone—whose identity I can guess —go to such lengths, staging a judicial appeal and casting you in the role of a widow?"

Her eyes seem to smile in the shadow of her veil.

"As surely as you live, my lord the king," she says, "no one can turn to the right or to the left from anything my lord the king says."

The twinkle fades from her eyes when my voice comes to a boom. "Isn't the hand of Joav with you in all this?"

"Yes, it was your servant Joav who instructed me to do this."

"What exactly did he ask you to do?"

Lowering her head, she quotes him. "'Pretend you're in mourning,' he said. 'Dress in mourning clothes, and don't use any cosmetic lotions. Act like a woman who has spent many days grieving for the dead.' Then he told me go to the court and speak these words, which he put into the mouth of your servant, before you."

"Why," say I. "What's his motive for doing such a thing?"

"Your servant Joav did this because he wants change."

"A change suggested by him must be carefully studied."

"He knows that your heart longs for your son, Absalom," she says, offering one more reason, just in case the first one has not been enough.

"How nice of him," say I.

To smooth things out, she uses her best tool: flattery. "My lord has wisdom like that of an angel of God. He knows everything that happens in the land."

"Apparently not," say I. "For a while there, you've managed to fool me."

"Only for a while," she says, "and only because you wanted to be fooled."

"Why on earth would anyone want to be fooled?"

"Perhaps for the chance to learn a tough lesson, so that you may become even wiser."

I rise from my throne and before she can warn her accomplice I rush to the door, which is where I pinch the end of that mustache, and say to the man attached to it, "Very well, Joav, I'll do it."

He does not stir, nor does he ask, Do what.

Without releasing him yet, "Go," I command. "Bring back the young man Absalom."

Joav falls with his face to the ground. He crawls about this way and that, trying to free himself from my hold. And with humility that is quite unusual for him, he grovels to me. He says, "Today your servant knows that he's found favor in your eyes, my lord the king, because the king has granted his servant's request."

Leaning over him I say, "Just make sure, for your own good, that you don't engage in such foolery as has been concocted by you today. Don't repeat it ever again, or else."

Joav dares not ask, Or else what.

He is so silent, in fact, that the only one I can talk to is myself. The conversation plays back and forth in my mind. It is all questions, questions with no answers. When Absalom comes back, shall I open my arms to him? Shall I kiss him? During these long months of exile, has he longed for me? Will he fall into my embrace? Will he cry? Will he ask forgiveness? Will he do it in earnest? Will he kiss me?

Even though I am about to let my son come back here, to my city, I cannot bring myself to face him, not yet. So much time has passed since I saw him, that something daunting and hard, something like an ocean has formed between us, a vast, icy ocean in which no life exists. It is made of frozen ripples, of things unsaid.

Of one fact I am certain: this is a new turn in the way my first in command relates to me. Given a chance to support some other leader, someone with a potential to become more resolute, more militant than me, Joav may join a revolt. But until then, he will refrain from arguing with me, even if he thinks me wrong.

I let go of my nephew, raise him to his feet, sensing that he is a bit shaken, which is a new thing. Never before was he afraid of me. I dust his knees and brush his mustache for him, so he is back to his old self, more or less.

Then I say, in the most decisive manner I can muster, "When you bring Absalom back here, he must go to his own house."

"But of course, your majesty," says Joav. "It's time to end his exile."

"Banished he shall remain," say I. "Absalom must not see my face."

The Prodigal Son
Chapter 9

And so, for the next couple of years, we live in the same city, my son and I, careful not to cross paths with each other.

At first he must have felt alone, disjointed from not only from me but also from the entire family, which brought upon him a severe sense of gloom. Having no sons to carry on the memory of his name Absalom took a pillar and erected it in the Kidron valley as a monument to himself. He named it after himself, and it is called Absalom's Monument.

But then, three sons have been born to him, and a daughter too. I have not seen her yet, but people tell me that she is endearingly sweet. He has named her Tamar, in honor of his sister, who has secluded herself in his house ever since the assault.

I long to see him—but in spite of myself I do not go to Absalom, nor do I allow him to come to me. The ice between us continues to harden. From time to time I ask myself, Why don't I reach over it to touch him? What is it I am waiting for?

And the only answer that comes close to sounding true is this: perhaps what I want is a proof of love. Even in my silence I need him to hear my heart, hammering madly inside me, aching for him. I yearn for him to care about me, care enough to kick the walls I have erected to separate us, so they burst open.

If that were to happen, everything will fall back into place. I can pardon him for his crime and name him my legitimate heir, in exchange for him taking both of us out of isolation and giving his children their grandfather back. Then, our family will be complete.

Meanwhile, time passes. One more spring is here. With the end of harvest time, throngs of people arrive here from every corner of the land, to celebrate the festival of Shavuot. By instituting this pilgrimage, which happens three times a year, I have turned the City of David into a spiritual center, as well as an economic hub.

Farmers and shepherds are pulling their wagons or riding their donkeys up the winding roads to Jerusalem, carrying sacks of wheat, bags of nuts, loads of fruits and vegetables, and meats of every kind. First they offer a sacrifice in front of the tabernacle of God, which is pitched at the top of the newly named Temple Mount. This is a site I have recently designated for a future temple.

Then they spread out around the city, to trade their produce for bread and drink. You see vendors all around the city, setting up stands at every street corner. You hear their voices ringing in every market, competing one against the other to reach the most ear-splitting, deafening volume. With great flair, they are praising the freshness of their produce or the quality of their merchandise, and announcing bargain prices which are only starting points for animated bargaining. They exchange ducks for cows, tomatoes for meat, flowers for furniture. The spirit of renewal is everywhere.

To entertain the masses I organize a huge parade. At the head of the royal procession, dancers are twirling their skirts about, actors are brandishing toy swords over their heads, musicians are blowing their trumpets, striking their cymbals, and beating their drums, all with intense rhythms that combine together to quicken the blood.

Standing in my golden chariot, here I arrive, with my two adorable young boys: Adonijah on my left and Solomon on my right. I hand them the reins, and teach them to guide the team of three horses at a steady trot.

"Don't tighten the reins," I tell Solomon, "or you'll lose control."

"I'm trying, dad," he says.

"I can do it," says Adonijah, trying to nudge me aside. "Here, let me show you!"

"Slow down! This is a breakneck pace," I tell him. "What's the rush, all of a sudden?"

"I'm impatient," he says.

"I can't do it, dad," says Solomon, handing the reins back to me.

I smile at his freckled face.

"No matter," I say. "Take your time. Meanwhile, wave to the people around you. Give each and every one of them a little nod."

And turning to Adonijah I say, "Look at all these people. Not so long ago they thought of themselves as members of different tribes, at odds with one another. Now we're all one nation. What you're watching is more than merely a parade. This, you see, is history in the making!"

"They're so happy," says Solomon, looking up to me.

"They're loving us," says Adonijah, glancing at them.

"Take it all in," I tell them. "Watch the horses. See the feathers crowning their heads bobbing as they trot. See the waves rolling with the wind along their manes, their tails. Enjoy the bright sparkle of the sun, sliding upon their skin with each movement. Hear the music, the blaring applause. This, boys, is a moment to remember."

A multitude gathers around us, cheering.

"What a perfect picture," says one. "This is what bliss looks like."

A second says, "I wish my kids would look up to me, just like that!"

"What a joy it is, simply to watch them, father and sons! So loving, so close together," says the third.

At the sound of that I bite my lips, so as to stop a sudden urge to cry. No matter. I lick the spurt of blood, and go on doing what I must. I smile through the tears, wave at everyone, bless men and women, and kiss the babies they hold out to me. All the while I scan all these figures, all these scarfs, handkerchiefs, veils, dotting the space around us with bright colors, near and far. Whenever I catch a glimpse of a shock of red hair amongst them, my heart skips a beat, hoping that perhaps it is Absalom.

Has he chanced to come? Is it him, peeking there between that shoulder and another? Is he wishing, perhaps, to stand right here, by my side, and enjoy this surge of excitement around us? Is he about to surprise me, step forward away from the rest of the spectators, and climb onto the chariot, so we may embrace each other, at long last, and cry together over lost time?

The chariot moves on. It turns a corner. The next street opens before us, and another one after that. New voices arise, calling out my name. Others fade behind us. I strain to separate the sounds, to find his voice in the clamor. All in vain.

Never once do I see his face.

Long ago I thought that the adoration bestowed upon me can never become unpleasant—but here I am, fatigued by it. So when I hear that the crowds have shifted the focus of their attention to someone else I find myself relieved, at first.

It does not alarm me in the least that their new idol is none other than my son, Absalom. Quite the contrary. With his gorgeous appearance, the luster in his green eyes, his hair, no one deserves to be loved more than him. Of all my children, he is the one I adore—even though he is a mystery to me. I do not want to believe that his crimes define him, and so I have no idea who he is.

I tell myself that after all, my son is an extension of me, my own flesh and blood, resurrected in a young body and an invincible spirit. I have already accepted in my mind that he should be the one to succeed me. He should carry forward the legacy of the House of David, in spite of the fact that he spurred his friends to execute my firstborn, Amnon. After a long exile, Absalom must have learned his lesson. I certainly hope so. At long last I am ready to forgive.

My two maidservants are talking behind my back as they change the bedsheets. Thinking that I have become too absentminded to notice them, they neglect to lower their voice.

"In all Israel," says the old maid, "there's not a man so highly praised for his looks as Absalom."

"So handsome," says the young one, with a little chuckle. "Cute, too!"

"From the top of his head to the sole of his foot there's not a blemish in him."

"Perfect, is what he is!"

"When his hair gets long, all the king's wives envy him for it —"

"And so do I! So shiny, so luxurious!"

"And when he cuts it—because it becomes too heavy for him —he weighs it, and its weight is two hundred shekels, by the royal standard."

"I'm going to save my pay, and buy me a curl of it."

"It's expensive," says the old maid. "Incredibly so!"

The young one giggles. She says, "What do I care about money? I'll put his curl in a trinket, and hang it on a chain over my heart, and show it all around town! It'll bring me lots of luck!"

"Now you'll have to wait, 'cause Abalom cuts his hair only once a year, during the feast of the sheering of the sheep."

At that, the young maid looks left and right, and then asks, in a hushed tone, "Isn't that when his brother, Amnon, was executed by his friends?"

"It is," confirms the old one.

"And now, now Absalom celebrates cutting his hair, on the very same date? If you ask me, that's a strange way to commemorate death in the family."

"No doubt. Strange it is."

"Often I wonder about him," says the young maid, dreamily. "He's so lovely to behold, but what's he thinking about, looking at himself so intently in the mirror, checking his profile this way and that, as his hair is being cut?"

The old one replies, "I bet he's thinking, 'Am I my brother's keeper?'"

"No, I don't think so. He wastes no time brooding over the past." The young maid hints at me. "The only one to do that is David."

"You're right. Absalom is taken by his plans for the future. Whichever way he decides to go, people will follow."

"I certainly will," says the young maid, with a sigh. "Oh my, I love him so."

"You're not alone," says the old one, coldly. "That young man seems to be falling in love with his own reflection."

*

One summer evening, thick smoke spreads across the city, as if it were under attack. A blaze leaps across one valley, then another. One structure after another bursts into flames. One field after another melts into liquid gold. Sparks shoot out every which way. From my chamber window you can barely see the horizon, where the hills of Jerusalem meet the sky, because the blue in them swirls around in the air, marred with charcoal gray. Nor can you detect where the fire may have started.

I summon my first in command, so he may call the troops, if he has not yet done so, and organize them into teams, to douse the flames with water, and to rescue the miserable souls caught in them.

Joav comes before me, fuming. His mustache is filled with gray particles that come flying out when he speaks.

"It's all under control," he says, even before I have a chance to ask anything.

"Is it?" say I. "Hard to tell, from here. Where did the fire start?"

Through clenched jaws he says something, some word that is utterly inaudible.

"Joav?" I demand, and look at him sternly, till at last he blurts out, with a puff of stuff flying out of his mouth, "In my field, my own barley field."

"Really? And what's the cause of it?"

In place of an answer he shuffles from one boot to another, rubs his charred hands together, and finally says, "Let me handle it. Can I go now?"

"Not until I get an answer out of you," say I.

"Life and property are at stake," he says. "I beg you, let me go! My soldiers are waiting—"

"So am I," I tell him, noting that they have been well trained to do what needs to be done. I see them out there, burning the dry brush, so that by the time the flames reach it they will have nothing more to consume.

He is silent, stubbornly so. I have never seen him so close to a breakdown.

"Joav," I say, "do I need to repeat myself?"

Absolutely livid, he shakes his head, No.

"So?" I prod him. "What, in heaven's name, is the cause of the fire?"

"Arson."

"Arson?" I echo, wondering who would dare set fire to the field of the most feared man in the land? Who would be so rude, so insolent as to threaten not only what belongs to Joav but also what belongs to me and to the entire city?

In our history we had a hero, Samson, notorious for being reckless. According to legend he caught three hundred foxes, turned them tail to tail, put a torch in the middle between two tails, and set it aflame. Then, he released the pairs of foxes into the standing grain of the Philistines. Their crops and standing grain, along with the vineyards and groves, were burnt to ashes.

Is this payback time? Are they still bitter over that old stunt? Why else would they target my own reckless military man? Is the era of peace about to come to an end? What does it mean, this scorching of our land? Are we already at war?

I demand, "Who is the culprit, d'you know? Who set your field aflame?"

Joav bites his lips, which makes me jump to the wrong conclusion. "Was it the Philistines?"

"The Philistines?" he repeats, surprise ringing in his voice. "Ha! I wish! Them I can handle, your majesty!"

"Who was it, then?"

"Your son."

"Who?"

"Absalom."

In utter confusion I mutter, "What? I don't believe it! "

"Believe it," says Joav, and starts spewing out black dust, along with some choice words for Absalom, which I am not going to repeat, as they are not worth mentioning.

"Well," say I. "I'm trying to be patient with you, but you're making it way too difficult. Will you tell me already what happened?"

"Absalom asked me to talk to you, to plead on his behalf," he says, "but I knew your wrath. I saw it with my own eyes, when I've tried to convince you, with the help of the wise woman of Tekoa, to bring him back. And so, I refused."

"Go on," I say. "I'm listening."

"Then your son sent for me a second time," says Joav. "Again I refused to come. And the next thing I know, he told his servants, 'Look, Joav's field is next to mine, and he has barley there. Go and set it on fire.'"

"This can't be happening," I say, shaking my head.

"Forgive me for saying this, your majesty: your son is unstable!" says Joav. "I didn't want to believe it at first—but now I do! He's utterly mad! I was hoping that one day, when he succeeds you, he'll heed my advice, and send our valiant warriors to battles on as many fronts as possible, which is what's needed, of course, to keep the peace—but then, how can I control a leader who is out of his mind?"

In reply I give him a look.

"I mean," he says, correcting himself, "how can I rely on him?"

"Too bad," say I. "I suppose you're stuck with me."

Joav fails to see the humor in all this. Instead he hisses, "Insane, insane, insane! That's what he is!"

I say, "Aren't you too harsh with him?"

And he says, "Ha! Doesn't he know who I am? He's made an mistake, a grave mistake to damage what I own! Who does he think he is, threatening me, burning my property?"

"He's my son."

"I swear, dearly will he pay for what he did!"

"What d'you mean?"

"Never again will I support him."

"That, I suppose, is not a bad thing."

"I did go to his house," says Joav, his gray blue eyes smoldering with hate. "And I asked him, 'Why have your servants set my field on fire?'"

"And? What did Absalom say?"

"He said to me, 'Look, I sent word to you and said, 'Come here so I can send you to the king to ask, Why have I come from Geshur? It would be better for me if I were still there!' To which I said, 'You might as well go back.' And he said, 'Damn you! I want to see the king's face, and if I am guilty of anything, let him put me to death.'"

Joav may not understand why a smile erupts on my face. Nor do I understand it, except to say that part of me enjoys hearing to what lengths my son has gone, simply to be brought into my court, to be accepted by me.

Is this not what I wished for? Did I not pray for a proof of his love, his caring for me? Is it not what he is giving me now, by violating every rule, every boundary set in place to separate between us?

Fire is roaring all around the palace, devouring whatever comes in its way. Am I mad? Why am I grateful for the hot, smoldering ground, thinking that this is what it takes to bring us together?

I try to persuade myself that there is a time for everything, and a season for every activity under the heavens. *A time to plant and a time to uproot what is planted. A time to kill and a time to heal. A time to tear down and a time to build up.*

I summon him, and he comes in and bows down with his face to the ground before me. Seeing him so close to me I am stunned. There is a change in him, which is hard for me to define, except to say that he is even more beautiful than he used to be, with that devilish glint in his eye.

My son leans towards me and fills his cheeks with air, as if in preparation for giving me a kiss—but it never leaves his lips.

In the end, unable to wait any longer, I am the one to give up. I succumb to my longing for him. Leaving the throne behind me I go down the stage, and embrace him.

I do not even care that my face is awash with tears as I kiss him. What burns me inside is that he does not return my kiss. Perhaps Absalom is too busy studying the curves of my empty seat—but then, I forgive him that, too.

The Edge of Revolt

Chapter 10

This winter I have fallen into the habit of wandering out to the roof, even if Bathsheba is not with me. Reclining on the cold tile floor I lean against the wooden lattice, right there at the edge, and lose myself in thought. Sometimes I take the crown off my tired head, and roll it across the dusty surface, glad that no one is watching me. I wonder then, why did I put so much effort, back in my youth, to grasp for it?

Perhaps I take it for granted these days. Like a bad coin, the thing always rolls back into my hand.

Between one wooden slat and another I survey the view. There, you can see Joav's barley field. In recent winters the rains have washed through it, bringing new growth that covers the scorched land. Next to it, a charred, hollow bark with frayed fibers is all that remains of an old olive tree. It is crumbling away, as new stems come shooting out of its gnarled roots. In the areas beyond, the flames must have stimulated the release of seeds, enriched the soil with wood ash, and removed competing plants. So all over the hills, young bushes, trees, and shrubs are flourishing with great vigor.

Out with the old, in with the new.

Four years have passed since the fire, four long years during which my heart is at peace, almost. My son is back, he is home! I got what I wanted, did I not? In an effort to rejoice at the thought of it I have tried not to think about his cold embrace, and about the hot air that came out of his mouth, in place of a kiss—but how can I forget it, when he is so generous with his kisses to everyone else but me?

With Gad the Seer becoming too frail, in his old age, to minister to my needs, a new adviser has joined the court. Zadok is a kind priest who, like his name suggests, it truly righteous. I may sound moody when talking to him—but only because he makes me feel at ease, so there is little need to pretend, or to shield my thoughts from him.

He brings out a heavy coat, bends over me, and places it carefully upon my shoulders.

"Your majesty," he says, "People are talking—"

"Who cares," I mutter. "Nothing good comes out of hearing what they say."

"It's about Absalom."

"Is it," say I, as dryly as I know how. "Even more reason to ignore idle gossip."

Zadok hesitates. He opens and closes his mouth several times, after which he says, "Your majesty?"

"What?" I grumble.

"It's about his ambition," he says.

"You mean, the excess of it?" I ask. "Is his ambition too much of a good thing?"

"Believe me, I don't want to be the one telling you this, but I think you must hear it."

"Must I?"

"Whenever anyone approaches him, your son reaches out his hand, takes hold of him and kisses him."

"How nice," say I, trying to bring a smile to my lips, and to my voice. In spite of me, it trembles with envy.

Meanwhile, the priest drones on. "Absalom," he says, "behaves like a politician, and worse: like a contender for the throne—"

"Being a prince," say I, "he's entitled."

Zadok looks at me as if to say, "Call it what you will, you can't explain this away! His behavior is a bit much, don't you think?"

Out loud he says, "Absalom behaves this way especially toward those who are on their way to the court, your majesty, to ask for your help, and for justice."

"Perhaps," say I, "he has a keen interest in the judicial system."

"You think he does?"

"I do, really," say I, trying to sound sure of myself, but my voice falters. "I mean, unlike my firstborn, who showed no interest in the office, Absalom seems to prepare himself for it. It's a good thing."

With a dubious tone, the priest says, "Perhaps so, your majesty."

To show confidence I raise my voice. "My son," I say, "is an extension of me. He will carry on my legacy."

"So much so," says Zadok, "that he wants to replace you already."

"Nonsense."

"He places himself between you and your subjects."

"Says who?"

"My lord, everyone knows it! He gets up early and stands by the side of the road leading to the city gate. Whenever anyone comes with a complaint to be placed before you, Absalom calls out to him, and starts with that smooth talk of his."

"Such as?"

"Such as, 'Look, your claims are valid and proper, but there's no representative of the king to hear you. If only,' says Absalom, "I were appointed judge in the land! Then everyone who has a case could come to me and I would see that they receive justice.'"

I chuckle. "Now here's a great idea, if I ever heard one! With his wits, he'll do great as a judge—"

"Will he?" asks the priest. "To do so, one must have respect for the law."

To which I say, "I know exactly what you mean. Absalom is guilty of murder and arson, but those blunders are now behind him, or so I hope."

The priest seems to be fighting an urge to raise an eyebrow. "Hope," he says, "is not enough. We're talking of the next king of Israel. Such blunders, as you call them—"

"They happened years ago, when he was still in his teens," say I, cutting in. "Have you never made mistakes in your life, in a moment of heat? I know I have."

"Murder and arson aren't mistakes. They're crimes."

"Which is why he spent two years in exile."

"Your majesty, I may be new around here," says the priest. "Please, be so kind as to tell me: is it just me who thinks you're too easy on him?"

"You're not alone," I admit. "In fact I think so too—but what can I do, other than pray that he's learnt his lesson?"

Zadok seems to hold himself back from shaking his head, yet in spite of him, it moves left and right, ever so slightly. "Your majesty, don't you see?" he asks. "Your son steals the hearts of the people of Israel."

"Why should it be his fault," say I, "if they're giving their hearts freely to him?"

"What he steals," says he, "is the admiration they used to feel towards you."

"Don't you get it? My son can't rob me of anything! He *is* me," I insist. "The best of me!"

Zadok hesitates to quibble with what I say.

"What they admire," I say, pointing vaguely at the city, "is me in him."

The priest cannot resist it any longer: he raises an eyebrow.

"I hope it's me who's mistaken," he says. "I so wish you were right."

*

In the course of time Absalom has stopped riding a mule, which is what all the rest of the princes are using for transportation. He claims it is a lowly, stubborn animal, not fit for his purposes, whatever those might be. Instead he has now provided himself with a chariot and horses, and with fifty men to run ahead of him.

From my chamber window I see him standing down there, at the head of his elegant vehicle. Carried forward, he looks achingly beautiful. His hair rides, waves upon waves, upon the wind, with curls large and small, furling and unfurling. It is a magnificent sight to behold.

With a strange blend of cruelty and tenderness he whips the horses and smiles to a multitude of his fans.

If that seems extravagant to you, consider this: I would give him a hundred, no—a thousand men to run ahead of him, if that would bring him closer to me. I would give him my own golden chariot, and my own team of horses, because I figure that given more gifts, he would have to show gratitude. Perhaps he would go as far as showing some warmth, some sign of affection for me.

I want him to settle down. The more things he amasses—the less rebellious he may become. Not that there is anything wrong with being a rebel, mind you. If anything, it proves that he has an independent tilt of mind. Even in that, Absalom takes after me!

So it is with a sense of pride that I say, under my breath, "Like father, like son."

This morning he comes into the court and bows before me. As usual I open my arms to him.

In place of a hug he opens his arms, as if to mirror what I do. Then he twirls around the court, arms stretched out, as if this were some foreign dance, the steps of which are unfamiliar to me.

I say, "Come here, son."

And he says, "Let me go to Hebron."

I am reluctant to do so, because his long exile left a chasm between us, a rift that to this day is difficult to bridge. I worry that letting him go may extend it ever farther.

So with a tremble in my lip I ask, "Why?"

"Because," he says. "I must fulfill a vow I made to the Lord."

In our culture, a vow is considered a serious thing, perhaps even sacred. I find myself blocked by it. There is no way for me to ask him to change his mind.

Still I think he can sense what I think, which is this: "I don't believe you. This, Absalom, is merely an excuse for some mischief, for which I already forgive you."

Compelled by my silence to offer more details, he says, "While your servant was living at Geshur I made this vow: 'If the Lord takes me back to Jerusalem I'll worship Him in Hebron.'"

"First," say I, "stop talking of yourself as my servant. We both know you're not. Next to me, you're the highest ranking man in this land. You're heir to the throne."

"And second?"

"Second," say I, with a catch in my throat, "why, why should you go elsewhere? People come from all around the country, on a pilgrimage to worship in Jerusalem. Since you were brought here, and the tabernacle of God is close, within a walking distance, why go to Hebron?"

"Why d'you have to ask so many questions?"

"Why can't you answer just this one?"

"A vow is a vow, is all I can tell you."

In truth I have never seen my son praying, nor have I ever witnessed him worshipping the Lord in any other way—but then, who knows? I admit I do not know him, not really. My son is a stranger to me.

I wonder, has Absalom ever felt a pang of remorse over what he did, I mean, fooling me into sending his brother to that horrific feast, that execution? Has he ever repented?

Is my son, like me, in search of redemption?

Out loud I say, "Go in peace," while thinking, "And in peace, come back to me."

Turning to go, he gives me a last look, with a sharp shine in those bright eyes of his. Then he lowers them, lest I read his mind.

I do not know why, but something in me hisses fear. This is an odd farewell. I sense that I will never meet him face to face again.

*

Absalom is out of my presence. As soon as I see his outline, standing there in his fancy chariot and whipping the horses that carry him out of the palace gate, my head clears, which is not a good thing. Alas, thinking brings doubts, and doubts bring pain, which starts to gnaw at me, sharper and sharper, to the point that I groan. I curse myself, sensing that I may have made a mistake.

It has to do with his choice of a place of worship, which seems utterly suspicious, because—how could I forget?—Hebron is a military stronghold.

I know, because I lived there seven long, dreary years, before conquering the City of David and making it my own. Being a provincial town Hebron was a perfect choice for me, at a time when I was considered a scoundrel and a traitor.

It was a safe base, a place to build up my defenses, because it belongs to my tribe, the tribe of Judah. And later, it was there that the elders anointed me king over them, which marked something new, a formal recognition of my political value, and of something else I brought them: hope.

The rest of the tribes took note, even though they continued to fight a misguided, bloody civil war against me. Unable to win it, and unable to deny that my first coronation was history in the making, they ended up submitting to my rule. I became king over all twelve tribes of Israel. News of this second coronation reverberated from Babylon in the north to Egypt in the south.

Nowadays, anything that happens in that place carries a symbolic significance to the entire nation, because several generations ago, it was there that Abraham, our legendary forefather, had purchased the Cave of the Patriarchs from the Hittites. His bones are deemed sacred. By extension, so is Hebron.

With a growing sense of trepidation I try to anticipate what my son is planning to do there.

And this is what I have come to realize: of all the things he knows about me, most of which he despises, here is one he is about to adopt: he will set up a coronation for himself, right there in Hebron, just like the one I had. And then, then he will come for me here, in my city, to make it his own.

It is with bitterness that I whisper, "Like father, like son."

I should have stopped him. I should have looked him in the eye, to show him that he can not fool me, not anymore.

"I shouldn't have let him go," I say to my bodyguard, Benaiah.

And to my surprise, he grasps what I mean at once. I do not have to spell things out for him, which is truly bad, because if he gets it, so does everyone in the city. Alas, my mistake must be common knowledge by now, as is the danger to my throne.

"No," he says, simply. "You shouldn't have."

Trying to sound casual I demand, "Any news? What's happening there, in Hebron?"

"I hear that Absalom sent messengers throughout the tribes of Israel."

"Did you catch any of them? D'you know what message they were carrying?"

Benaiah scratches his head. "The one I caught," he says, "had a scroll in his hand."

"And? What did it say?"

"Here." He hands the thing to me. "I don't know what it's about, and the messenger wouldn't tell me either, because, he said, it's a secret."

"Not anymore," say I, breaking the seal.

I note that the signature pressed into it is of a new design. It carries the first letter of son's name, done in ornate, flamboyant curves.

At this point, it does not surprise me to read what is has been delivered to the elders of all the tribes, and what amounts to a call to arms against me. "As soon as you hear the sound of the trumpets, then cry out, 'Absalom is king in Hebron.'"

In the next few hours I get more updates about the revolt. My first in command, Joav, tells me that hundreds of men, who have followed Absalom from Jerusalm to Hebron, are invited to attend what they think is a religious event, complete with praying and offering a sacrifice. They may not know the full plan of this celebration—but I expect my son to anoint himself right there, in their presence, maybe as soon as tonight.

I learn one more thing: Absalom has sent for Ahithophel the Gilonite, my own counselor, to come from Giloh, his hometown. Ahithophel is one of the smartest men I know. His son is Eliam, father of my wife Bathsheba, which is why I trusted him until now, as if he were my own blood, my family.

Now I recall that following the death of Bathsheba's first baby, and the scandal surrounding our affair, Ahithophel seemed to distance himself from me. He stopped volunteering his advice freely, as he had done before. And lately, he has been especially tight lipped. Even when I asked for his opinion, he would not give it.

I have no doubt that with his support, the conspiracy will gain strength, and its following will go on increasing.

Meanwhile my scribe, Gad the Seer, has passed away quietly in his bed. In the past I resented the zeal with which he used to pursue every little affair I was involved in, so he may record it in his scriptures—but now I feel sorry to lose his counsel.

In coming days I must go back to surviving by my wits, and by sorting out the best tips, given by my longtime advisors.

Losing two of them in one day—one due to treachery, the other due to natural causes—makes this task all the more daunting.

And so, by the end of the day, when a messenger comes to tell me, "The hearts of the people of Israel are with Absalom," I realize the full meaning of these words. There are two kings in the land.

One of them must be toppled.

It is then that I mourn for my scribe, Gad the Seer. These tears are also meant for me, and for the end of an era.

I imagine his long, ghastly finger wagging at me, and hear his voice bleating faintly, out of some fold in my memory. He is uttering those harsh, ominous words, "The sword will never depart from your house, because you despised me, and took the wife of Uriah the Hittite to be your own."

Refusing to surrender to his prophesy I grasp the hilt of Goliath's sword, and brandish it in the air once or twice, against an invisible enemy. Against my son.

Then, laying it down at my feet and brushing my fingers against the sharp blade I ask myself, Am I done? Is it time to give in?

Lost in doubts I go out to the roof, where only last night I have taken the crown off my tired head, and rolled it across the surface. That, I vow, will never happen again. I am a king, and a king I shall remain till my last breath.

Out with the old, in with the new?

Searching deep in me, the only answer I find is, No! Not this way! I cannot allow my legacy to erode, merely to entertain my son's greed, his lust for power. I have worked too hard at building this city, uniting this nation, and changing the course of history in this land.

His threat only awakens the fighter in me.

Departure

Chapter 11

At this hour I know what is coming. I feel it in my bones. When a new hero rises, people will follow him anywhere, even to the demise of their old hero, the one they so admired as long ago as yesterday. I sense it, and so does Absalom.

To take advantage of their adoration—which, as he knows, is a fleeting thing—my son must act swiftly. He must seize the moment and lead the revolt against me, take it out of the provincial city of Hebron and into the center of our nation, the City of David. In his mind, one of us must die. He is preparing himself to force me into my grave.

His mission is simple: slay me. By contrast, mine is inherently more complex: survive, and protect him from being slain by the few who still remain loyal to me. To do so I must avoid an outright clash between our forces.

Given my hesitation to act in recent years, ever since the rape of my daughter, Tamar, and the murder of my son, Amnon, you may expect me to go into a long give and take with myself, weighing the moral value and the possible impact of one alternative over another. But no! To my surprise, this time I arrive at my decision in a snap.

According to my calculations, my son will be storming into the gates of Jerusalem, followed by the riffraff, by sunrise. If I stay in my city, which is ill-prepared for urban warfare, I may win in the end, at the cost of its total destruction. And so I know what must be done. Hours before he comes I must be gone.

There is little time left.

Every moment is crucial. In spite of this, there is one task I must complete right now, before my departure. I must defend something far dearer to me than life: my legacy, which my son is sure to obliterate, in his push to topple me into oblivion.

Tonight of all nights, the guards at the door have fallen asleep. Inside, the court seems empty. The flame has gone out of the torches left and right of the stage, where my throne is set. My pulse is quickening, as always in the presence of danger. I look left and right, and by the faint rays of the moon I find my way, as stealthily as I can, to the central glass display.

I sort through the numerous historical records in it, lift up a few selected scrolls, and leave the rest of them in place. Just for good measure I throw in a few blank ones, which I arrange neatly, to give the appearance that nothing has gone missing.

I glance over my shoulder. No one is present, except the head of Goliath in the next glass display. My pebble is still firmly lodged in his forehead, which continues to crack, ever so slightly, from one year to another. By the moonlight, he seems more pale than ever. I imagine that to him I may look like a common thief.

"Trust me," I whisper, raising the scrolls to his eyes, as if to gain the approval of an old friend. "I'm taking these for both of us. The story of our encounter should live on. It shouldn't disappear, which is what is sure to happen, when my son takes control of this place."

Set upon the severed neck, the head of Goliath seems to express uncertainty. So I go on to tell him, "I can just hear my son, proclaiming, 'Written material is dangerous! It makes you think! If you have it, better give it to me for safe disposal.' His soldiers will collect every piece of papyrus left behind, throw it into a big heap, and set it ablaze."

Behind the glass Goliath seems to flash a look at me out of those shadows, deep down the sockets of his eyes—or else the wink I see is merely a reflection of mine.

Perhaps, like me, he imagines the valley of Ellah, where we first met, years ago. I remember: it opened ahead of me like a fresh cut. Thin, muddy streams were washing over its rocks, oozing in and out of its cracks, and bleeding into its soil. Layers upon layers of moist, fleshy earth were pouring from one end to another, then halting on a slant, about to slip off. And from down below, somewhere under the heavy mist that hid the bottom of the valley from sight, stirred some unexpected sounds. In place of the first birdsongs of the day, there rose the shrieks of vultures.

On that note I tell myself, There is little time left.

I take the scrolls and layer them, with great care, at the bottom of a leather satchel, which I place in an empty clay pot that stands just past the sleeping guard, out in the courtyard. It has no decorations, and no identifying marks on it. What it does have is a heavy lid, which I tighten in place with some glue, so as to preserve the scrolls in a dry, cool condition. I hope no one heard it squeak.

Who knows if I will ever come back to Jerusalem, if I will have a chance to recover these scrolls—but maybe, sometime in the future, someone else will.

I carry the pot to the house of my court historian, Gad the Seer. Inside, lying upon the bare table, shrouded in white, his body is ready for tomorrow's funeral.

The professional mourner hired for this occasion, an old woman with no teeth, stirs out of her sleep. She raises her head, which is utterly bald with the exception of a single stand of hair. In her confusion, she starts the obligatory wailing.

"Shush, lower your voice," I tell her. "Save it for tomorrow, when they inter him."

She rasps something, but it is hard to understand what comes out of that black mouth of hers, when she is not wailing.

"This," I say, pointing, "is one thing that was dear to him."

Her voice rises again. "A pot?" she cries.

"Hush," say I. "You don't want to wake the dead, do you?"

She waves her knuckled hand. "Wake him?" she screeches. "Ah, he's stone cold!"

"Too bad," say I. "He can't appreciate the lovely rhythms of your voice, sometime sobbing, sometime slobbering over him."

"You making fun of me?"

"Not at all! You're the best at what you do."

"Of course," she says, relaxing into a toothless smile. "I'm a professional."

And I say, "Even the king can't project sound quite the way you do."

And she says, "He should come to me! I can teach him a thing or two."

"I bet you can," say I. "Now do me a favor: make sure they place this thing next to Gad's body, down in the crypt."

With greed in her eyes, she says, "Why would he need it?"

"Because," say I, "in the afterlife—"

"Ah, there's no such thing!"

"Well, no one ever came back to tell us that, did they?"

"If you have doubts," she says tersely, "keep them to yourself."

To which I say, "What I have is hopes—"

"Doubts, hopes, what's the difference? I deal with what's certain, such as death." To prove her point she raises her hand, which is covered with ropy veins, and with a strange sort of glee she slaps Gad the Seer across his cheek, full force. "See?" she croaks. "He can't even bat an eye! Ah, dead as a doornail!"

"I suggest you step away from the deceased—"

"You afraid I'll hurt him? Ah! Nonsense!"

"He was a man of God, so you could use some respect—"

"What I can use is that pot! Give it to me! I'm not paid nearly enough for the effort I put in!"

"This clanky thing?" say I. "The lid wouldn't open, see? For you, it's useless, which is why we must leave it for the dearly departed."

She struggles to open it, in vain.

Hoping that the lid will continue to hold tight under her bony fingers I tell her, "Why would you need anything that must be broken to pieces before you can reach inside?"

"Fine, into the crypt it'll have to go," she mutters. "Let Gad keep an eye on the clanky old thing!"

"How fitting," I say, under my breath. "His entire life he was the keeper of history. Let him continue to guard it."

On my way out I try to penetrate the mystery of the future. I imagine a pair of lovers, looking for a secluded place where they can cuddle together, away from the watchful eyes of their families. I see them descending, hand in hand, under the stone floor of a long forgotten burial vault. There, in the shadowy crypt, they may stumble upon this clay pot, and unearth its contents. I hope that for them, history will remain readable.

*

Back in my chamber I cast a quick look around me. With all the expensive things in my treasure box, all the crowns and jewels and stuff, there is nothing here I wish to take on the road with me. For a chance to stay alive I must be light on my feet, and these objects, which I have accumulated over the years, are nothing but a burden. They will slow me down into a defeat.

The only things I am sorry to leave behind are my inkwell, and my quill. Perhaps I should leave a few last words, meant for Absalom, so he may find them when he breaks into my chamber to make it his own.

I find this idea incredibly tempting. And yet, staring at the blank papyrus I find the challenge of writing more daunting than ever. How can I admit to him, and to any other stranger who may lay a hand upon this note, what it feels to be undermined, to be betrayed by the one dearest to me?

I cannot do it. Instead I scribble something that obscures and reveals what I feel, in equal measure. *"Lord, how many are my foes! How many rise up against me!"*

What my son has leveled against me is a deeply personal offense. By now it has become a public spectacle, committed in front of the entire nation, so everyone can watch my humiliation, and my fall.

Words quiver on my lips. They scramble over the papyrus, bleeding ink. Choked with tears I try to sing them. *"If an enemy were insulting me I could endure it. If a foe were rising against me I could hide. But it is you, a man like myself, my companion, my close friend, with whom I once enjoyed sweet fellowship at the house of God, as we walked about among the worshipers."*

I blot the corner of my eye and remind myself, There is little time left. Even so I choose to spend a few more moments here, simply to take care of my writing instrument. I wash the ink off it with water from the jug. I wipe it carefully, feeling the lovely tingle of the feather upon my skin. And in parting I pass it between my lips, kissing its sharp tip.

And I murmur, Thank you. I am so grateful for the inspiration you have given me. I am blessed. If I am captured tomorrow I will die a happy man. So few are as lucky with their weapon as I have been.

At midnight I summon my officials, and tell them, "Come! We must flee, or none of us will escape from Absalom."

They wipe their sleepy eyes, wondering if this is some kind of a late night joke, or if this is real.

One says, "Did I hear correctly? You want us to escape?"

Another shakes his head. "No," he says. "This can't be! If this is truly an attack, then we should put up a fight!"

"That's what Absalom expects us to do," say I. "He's ready. We're not. So we must gain time, by confounding him. The palace must be vacated at once. Without any resistance to overcome, capturing it will disappoint him. In the absence of valiant fighting, his victory will be an empty one."

"Ah! It'll be nothing worth boasting about," says one, "or recording in the books."

"I think I get it," says the other.

And a third one says, in a shaky voice, "What I get is that I need more thinking."

"No," say I. "There's no time for that."

They look at each other, and shuffle from one foot to another instead of rushing out to awaken their staff and their wives, and get some provisions for the journey, such as winter coats, without which they may not survive the chill in the mountains of Judea.

"We must leave, now," I tell them.

"You mean, right this minute? Why?"

"Because," say I, "Absalom will be at the gates of the city at dawn. He'll move quickly to overtake us, and bring ruin upon our families, and put the city to the sword."

At last, my officials answer, "Your servants are ready to do whatever our lord the king chooses."

Urging my officials to prepare for departure has been the easy part. Now comes the hard one: dealing with my wives. When I arrive at the women's quarters, there is already a great commotion inside.

In a fit of excitement Abigail grabs an armful of scarves, skirts, aprons, coats, and dresses, and heaps them into a bed sheet, which is bulging to the point that it is impossible to bundle up. Michal hops about on one shoe, searching frantically for the matching one, and for her chandelier earrings. Abital stuffs as many rings and bracelets as can be concealed comfortably in her cleavage, and then some.

Bathsheba tries to wrap Solomon in a blanket despite his resistance. His brother, Adonijah, pokes him in his ribs and makes fun of him for being immature. Meanwhile Maachah, Eglah and Haggith are exchanging the latest fashion tips, as a way to figure out what to wear and what not to wear for the journey.

Meanwhile, a few concubines just stand there, on the other end, as if they are attached somehow to the place, and unable to figure out how to leave things behind, things that remind them of this or that moment in the past, and things they may well need, one day in the distant future.

"Lets go," I tell them. "There's no time to sort things out."

Maachah says, in her Geshurite accent, "Really? You can't be serious!"

While Bathsheba asks, "What should we take with us?"

And I say, "The kids."

And Michal asks, "Anything else?"

And I cry, "No! Enough already! Let's go!"

"What is this, all of a sudden? A rehearsal for exodus?" says Maachah. "Trust me, dear, you're no Moses!"

"No," say I. "And I can't bring you to the promised land, either, because as you know, you're already there."

"This is it?" she says, with a tone of dismay, while pointing vaguely around her, at the rich decor of the place, for which so much of the treasure has been spent. "For this," she says, acidly, "I had to cross the desert? Back in my father's palace, in Geshur, I expected so much more of you!"

I bite my lips. If not for this attitude, perhaps she would have found a way to raise her son, Absalom, with more respect towards me. Perhaps then, he would not be plotting to overthrow me now. Instead he would be waiting patiently for my passing, like any reasonable son in any normal family.

I breathe not a word of all this to her, because Maachah would see it as an accusation, and naturally there would be no argument that she is right.

"Well? Why don't you answer me?" She pokes me in my ribs. "I said, 'Is this the promised land?'"

"It is," say I. "And if you disapprove of it, I have a suggestion: let's get out of here as fast as our feet can carry us. We must leave, right now!"

Out of the corner, "I won't," says the oldest concubine, setting her hands upon her hips.

"And neither would I," says the youngest one. She sticks her fingers in her ears, so as not to hear the tumult in this place, and not to be a part of the excitement of it all. Then she turns over in her bed.

"Fine," say I, throwing my hands in the air. "Stay here, and keep the place tidy. I'm sure Absalom will appreciate it. And if he doesn't, don't complain to me about it!"

With that I march out of the woman's quarters. My wives are following me, all of them except ten of the concubines who are too attached to the luxuries in the palace. Solomon, Adonijah, and the rest of my children are trudging in the back.

By instinct, all of us know to keep quiet. Instead of going out through the palace gates I lead the way through the back exit, around the stables, where the stable boys are asleep, or so I hope. We climb out of the royal gardens through a fence, and tiptoe from there, careful not to make any noise that might wake anyone up. By now, no one expects chariots to carry us out, or horses, or even mules.

A cold wind is blowing in my face. I glance over my shoulder at my wives, who are fighting to advance against it. What have we become? Where am I leading these shadowy figures? How can a homeless man provide for those who cling to him?

I am not a young man anymore. Having gained some weight in recent years, my body is not as agile as it used to be. I ache with every step. I feel every stone, every pebble underfoot—but try as best as I can not to show it. My heart is heavy with doubt. How can I survive in the wilderness?

In a blink, the tears come.

Remove your scourge from me
I am overcome by the blow of your hand.

I do not want to look back, to see the silhouette of my palace. I want it to be swallowed at once into the vacuous blackness behind me, as if it never existed. Perhaps then I will not have to grieve for what I have lost.

Violence and Strife in the City

Chapter 12

This revolt, mounted by my own flesh and blood, forces me to consider my friends, advisors and military personnel with a degree of caution, and wonder who amongst them is a friend, and who—a foe. Before taking a risk and reaching out to any of them I must get a sense of their level of support for me. Are they devoted to my cause, which is to make this country not only strong but also stable? In my house, the House of David, there should be a peaceful transition of power from one generation to the next.

I send messages to a handful of people, calling them to meet me under the oak tree, on the other side of the ravine. Then I head in that direction with my wives. When we finally get there by the end of the day I note that Bathsheba has blisters on her heels. She is wincing in pain, as do the others. Back in the palace, where we used to walk on the softest of rugs, our soles have softened. Spoiled by luxury, so have our souls. To survive this winter in the wilderness, body and spirit must harden.

Can we do it? God knows.

The storm has subsided into an occasional gust that slaps the oak tree and makes its branches sigh. The old shred of garment, which as I recall must have belonged to my daughter, Tamar, is still clinging, somehow, to the highest branch, still twisting in the wind. By now there are more holes in it than threads, as if to remind me to figure out the missing matter in my own life.

I see more gaps in it than connections. When did the string of disasters start? Was it her rape, years ago? Was it the murder of my son, Amnon? Or else, was it my own sin, making love to Bathsheba and sending her husband, Uriah, to his death?

The first man to answer my call is Ittai the Gittite. He reminds me of Goliath—with two exceptions: first, he is big, but not quite as gargantuan, and second, his head is firmly attached to his body. Ittai is a Philistine general whom I hired only yesterday to be in charge of a legion of mercenaries, made up of three groups of Philistines: the Gittites, the Kerethites, and the Pelethites. If you think these are my enemies, think again. I would trust my life to them sooner than I would trust it to some members of my own tribe. Why? Because they have no tribal loyalties, which cause manipulation and scheming.

Some of these mercenaries used to live in the city of Gath, and some—in the city of Ziklag, which was given to me by Achish king of Gath. Serving him cost me my reputation, as my own people branded me an outcast and even worse, a traitor—yet it helped me forge a lasting alliance with these Philistines.

They saw themselves as belonging to me, and served me long before my rise to power, which may explain why to this day they remain faithful to me, even in my present predicament, which is not all that different from the one back then, in the past.

Ittai the Gittite removes his bronze armor, sets aside his long spear, and kneels before me, even though I am not a king anymore.

Just to test his loyalty I ask, "Why should you come along with us? Go back and stay with my son, Absalom. He's the king now!"

In reply he says, simply, "I'm yours."

"You're a foreigner, an exile from your homeland," say I. "You came only yesterday. And today, shall I make you wander about with us, when I don't even know where I'm going?"

"Wherever you go," he says, in his Philistine accent, "I'll go with you."

Even though I need his support, I pretend to refuse him a third time. "Go back, and take your people with you," I tell him. "May the Lord show you kindness and faithfulness."

Ittai is visibly moved to hear me bless him. His reply is more lengthy this time, and full of zeal. "As surely as the Lord lives," he vows, "and as my lord the king lives, wherever my lord the king may be, whether it means life or death, there will your servant be!"

Since my escape from my own palace I felt utterly destitute. I felt deserted—until now. So I embrace him, feeling grateful to accept his warmth. In exchange, the big man gives me a hearty pat on the shoulder. It nearly knocks me off my feet.

"Come," I say, beaming broadly. "Let's march on."

My old priest, Zadok, arrives here next, and then old Abiathar, heading a group of Levites, who are walking gingerly between one rock and another, carrying an incredibly precious object: the Ark of God. Behind them are their sons, Ahimaaz son of Zadok, and Jonathan son of Abiathar. And behind them is a long procession of people who are flocking to me, or perhaps escaping the upcoming unrest in the city. Either way I am touched.

But more than that I am horrified. Looking at the Levites I am amazed that the Levites have made it this far. My heart is aflutter, because I worry that one of the them may stumble into a pit or over a stone, which may tip the Ark. It may slip from their hold and then, then we may risk the wrath of God. Trying to mollify my fear I tell myself that things can go no worse than they already are.

They set the Ark down, and Abiathar offers sacrifices on a makeshift altar until all the people have finished leaving the city. It is a long ceremony, one that marks a farewell from the City of David and the end of an era.

Ahead of us is a barren mountain range, and the unknown. Under such harsh conditions I doubt that the priests can make it, because Zadok is old and frail, and so is Abiathar. If they insist on joining us, they will slow us down and become a liability.

So I tell them, "Take the Ark of God back into the city."

"We'll do no such thing," says Zadok.

And Abiathar shakes his head too, or perhaps it is merely a sign of his age.

So I say, in a manner that may be easy for them to accept, "If I find favor in the Lord's eyes, He will bring me back and let me see it and his dwelling place again. But if He says, 'I am not pleased with you,' then I am ready. Let Him do to me whatever seems good to Him."

The priests just stare at me, dumbfounded.

So I press on. I ask, "D'you understand? Go back to the city, with my blessing."

At last Abiathar relents. "Perhaps we can be of more help to you there," he says. "We may be able to send word to let you know the news from the palace."

"Take your son Ahimaaz with you, and also Abiathar's son Jonathan. They're good runners, are they not?"

"The best," says Zadok, with great fatherly pride.

"I'll wait at the fords in the wilderness," say I, "until word comes from you to inform me."

So Zadok and Abiathar lead the Levites on the journey back to Jerusalem. Watching them shrink away into the distance, with the Ark of God the last thing visible before darkness comes, I wonder if I will ever see them again.

There is no word back from my first in command, Joav, nor from the wisest of my advisors, Ahitophel. Rumors are that he is among the conspirators with my son, Absalom. I pray that his counsel may turn into foolishness—but knowing his exceptional wit I suppose that there is little chance of that.

Meanwhile, heavy clouds gather overhead, as if to press down on us. Only a single ray of sun penetrates, somehow, through them, illuminating the sadness that has fallen upon my followers. They begin to cry, like children, lost. The whole countryside seems to sigh, even to weep aloud as they pass by.

I cross the Kidron Valley, taking note of the caves, opening above us like misshapen eyes, with a wet shine that captures the last glint of sunlight, before everything goes dark.

I remember passing here before, years ago, in the opposite direction. At that time I was climbing up through the water shaft to storm the city, and make it mine.

Rain begins to wash over us, one glassy sheet after another. I keep looking ahead to find a path, seeing nothing but a reflection of me as a young boy, ready for adventure. I remember being in his skin, fighting, loving, dancing with all my might. Now I imagine myself crossing right through my own ghost. Perhaps there is a touch, a light touch between us, and a moment later I am reborn, old.

I feel a gust of air as the younger me fades away completely, and here I am, alone and dejected, helpless to read a path in the stars, because none are seen.

It is then, with a heart laden with worry, that I try to give it words. I chant them in a low voice as I go down into the darkest of the dark shadows.

How long, Lord? Will you forget me forever?
How long will you hide your face from me?
How long must I wrestle with my thoughts
And day after day have sorrow in my heart?
How long will my enemy triumph over me?

*

The next morning is a clear, sunny day, which in an odd way makes my anguish much more difficult to bear. Wildflowers pop over the hills, and fill the air with their sweet fragrance. Alas, even nature seems to ignore me, ignore the mood I am in! A full blown tempest would have been so much better!

I begin climbing up the Mount of Olives, weeping as I go. My head is covered, and I am barefoot. I know that grieving over my life may be a pitiful sight to you, but what of it? Do not judge me until you find yourself in my shoes. I mean, barefoot. I mean, without a reasonable chance for survival. Without hope.

Just listening to my own moaning I worry that it may disclose our location. The last thing I need is to be captured. Still, I cannot bring myself to stop.

My followers cover their heads too. They are weeping with me, raising the pitch of their sobs higher and higher as we climb up. When I arrive at the summit, where people used to worship God, I see a tall, wiry figure by the side of the road. My adviser, Hushai the Arkite, is there to meet me. His grief is even more pronounced than anyone else around me, as his robe is torn and there is dust on his head.

Seeing him I stop moping. I tell him outright, "If you go with me, you'll become a burden. But if you return to the city, you may be of help to me."

He understands me at once, and asks, simply, "How?"

"Go to Absalom," I say. "Tell him, in your most flattering tone, 'Your Majesty, I'll be your servant. I was your father's servant in the past, but now I'll be yours.' Then you can help me by frustrating Ahithophel's advice."

"That," says my confidant, "I can do. No one is better than me at sounding sincere."

"Don't I know it!" say I. "Sometimes I mistrust you when you're too nice to me."

"You should! I'm not a nice man, but a wily one."

"That's exactly the kind of man I need."

Hushai pleats his forehead. "Now, when I'm in the city, and you're out somewhere here, on your journey, how will I manage to warn you of your son's moves?"

I answer by asking, "Won't the priests Zadok and Abiathar be there with you? They're loyal to me. Tell them anything you hear in the palace."

"And their two sons, Ahimaaz son of Zadok and Jonathan son of Abiathar, are there with them?"

"They are. Send them to me with anything you hear."

Just then I sense, through my bare feet, a rumble shaking the earth. I know what it means, and by the fear in his eyes, so does my confidant. There is no need for words, when the sound of many hooves is speaking to us. Absalom is close. He is riding, perhaps as close to us as the other side of the mountain, at the head of his newly formed cavalry. The roar we hear is rolling forward, into the city.

I climb up to the summit of the Mount of Olives, hoping to catch sight of my son. I wonder if he chooses a roundabout way through the terrain, or if he goes for the water shaft, to storm the city from within, the same way I did.

But once I get to the top, there is no sign of him or his army. From here I have a clear view of my palace. The towers beacon me from afar. The rooftop outside my chamber is glistening in the morning sun. The wall hugging the city seems intact. I cannot see the gates, as they are on the other side of the hill, but I am certain that by now, Absalom has forced them open.

I am surprised that my first in command Joav has failed to arrive ahead of the others, or for that matter, he has failed to arrive at all. Instead, just beyond the summit, there stands another man. I know him. This is Ziba, the steward of Saul's grandson, Mephibosheth. He has a string of donkeys saddled and loaded with loaves of bread, cakes of raisins and figs, and a skin of wine.

Surprised to see these gifts I ask him, "Why have you brought these?"

"The donkeys are for the king's household to ride on," he says. "The bread and fruit are for the men to eat, and the wine is to refresh those who become exhausted in the wilderness."

"And your master's grandson?" I ask, avoiding the name because it is ridiculously long. "Where's he?"

"He's staying in Jerusalem, because he thinks, 'Today the people will restore to me my grandfather's kingdom.'"

I cannot help but laugh.

"Is that right?" I ask. "There's nothing better than calamity to unmask those who pretend to be friends. That boy has been eating at my table all these years!"

Ziva bites his lips, so as not to say, "And he hated every moment of it."

I shrug. "He knew I was keeping an eye on him, because he belongs to the House of Kish. Of course he hated it!"

"He calculates that the revolt may benefit him."

"That is proof that he's not only a danger to me, as I've thought he would be, but also far from being halfway bright. His grandfather's kingdom, in his dreams! Absalom, my rebellious son, has no intention of crowning anyone but himself."

"No question about that."

I make an effort to pronounce the name correctly, so there would be no question when I teach the boy a little lesson for both his folly and his disloyalty. "All that belonged to your master, Mephiboshet," I tell the steward, "is now yours."

"I humbly bow," says Ziba. "May I find favor in your eyes, my lord the king."

At that I ask myself, Am I, still? What does it mean, to rule an empire while at the same time, to wander about the country without a home, let alone a palace?

*

A light morning breeze carries new sounds to me. I run back to the summit to cast a look at my palace, and what do I see there, but hordes of wild, rowdy men coming out of the doors of my chamber, breaking them. They shout something incoherent, and brandish their weapons overhead, while kicking the wooden lattice that used to mark the edge of the roof. Some splintered slats dangle over the edge, some fall down the tower, bouncing against the stone treads of the outer staircase.

Meanwhile down in the courtyard, ten figures clad in what looks like puffy dresses are being pushed around by other soldiers, then forced up the stairs to escape being beaten. I cannot recognize them, not only because of the distance but also because they cower, and cry, and hang their heads between their shoulders, in fear of the pointed swords aimed at them from below, and of the falling debris from above.

The more I focus, the more I become convinced that these are the ten concubines I left behind, those who chose to stay in the palace, the night of my departure. I should have known better. I should have insisted that they come with me.

I am not the only one watching this spectacle. On one rooftop after another throughout the city, in this balcony and that, people gather to see what is about to happen up there to these women.

And then, in front of this huge audience, a man with a magnificent, reddish mane of hair steps out onto the rooftop. Taking center stage my son fills his chest with air, and utters the longest of roars, letting everyone know how victorious, how invincible he thinks he is.

It is then, at the sound of his screeching voice, that I know, without a doubt, what advice he has received from Ahitophel. "Sleep with your father's concubines whom he left to take care of the palace. Then all Israel will hear that you have made yourself hated to your father, that you have crossed the line, and that things will never return to the way they were. When you have done it, the hands of everyone with you will be more resolute."

Working with an odd mix of haste and anticipation, the men pitch a tent for Absalom right there, close to the edge, next to the shattered slats of wood. One woman after another is pushed onto the roof. One after another is brought to her knees at the opening of the tent. I cannot believe my eyes, watching my son as he is forcing himself on my concubines, in the sight of all Israel.

My heart breaks for them, and for all of us.

How have we come to this, my son and I? The reason he hates me so is that I failed to punish the man who assaulted his beloved sister, Tamar. From that day on Absalom blamed me for my inaction, which caused him to avenge her rape. And now, to celebrate his rise to power, he resorts to executing the very same crime—only in broad daylight, ten times over, molesting the bodies of ten innocent women who, just like his sister, are at a loss to hide their disgrace.

Even if this is meant to be a political move aimed to prove me a has-been, I know that it is changing him inside. In a most profound sense, he will never be the same. Feasting on violence Absalom has cracked. Before the entire nation he is turning insane.

I cover my ears and close my eyes. I am in tears.

Lord, confuse the wicked, confound their words
For I see violence and strife in the city.
Day and night they prowl about on its walls
Malice and abuse are within it.
Destructive forces are at work in the city
Threats and lies never leave its streets.

Scorned by Everyone

Chapter 13

I go down the Mount of Olives and approach Bahurim, which is where the road takes a sharp turn into the Jordan valley. Upon getting there I notice that my first wife, Michal, gives me a look.

"What?" I say.

And she says, "I know this place. I remember it."

And I say, "Do you?"

And she says, "Indeed. This is where I saw Paltiel for the last time."

It has been a long time since I heard the name of the man she had married in my absence, during my stay with the Philistines. That name was not to be spoken in my presence, ever since the princess was brought back to my court, by force. So the mention of it now is a sign that she uses my fragile political state to show me how little she cares about my feelings.

I am told her husband was heartbroken when I sent the Benjamite general, Abner, to take her from him, and bring her back to me.

"The most tragic thing is not having to part with your love," I suggest to her, "but having to stay with him."

"You're right about that," she retorts. "Still, you should've seen his face."

I shrug. "Never met him."

Michal sets her hands on her hips, and tells me, "I know what you would've told him, had you met."

"What would that be?"

"You would've said, 'What's mine is mine, and since I'm the king, what's yours is mine, too."

"No." I shake my head, for emphasis. "The only thing I would've asked him is, 'D'you hear same sweet nothings I keep getting from your wife, I mean, from my wife?'"

"Like what?"

"Like, 'You don't deserve me.'"

"Well, what can I do?" The princess rolls her eyes. "You don't!"

And with that, she goes back to join my other wives, way in the back of the line behind me.

I recall that Paltiel went with her, and wept behind her in public in the most ridiculously miserable way, wailing and moaning and howling, making a complete fool of himself all the way to this very place. At the time I had a hearty laugh with Abner, who escorted her all the way to my compound, at the expense of the poor fellow—but now I find myself here, at the same turn of the road, crying bitter tears.

This place must have a curse on it. Perhaps it is here to remind me not to laugh at the misery of others, or it will be visited on me.

Dogs surround me, a pack of villains encircles me.
They pierce my hands and my feet.
All my bones are on display.
People stare and gloat over me.
They divide my clothes among them, and cast lots for my garment.

And now it is at this turn that I am taught a tough lesson about mockery. A man from the same clan as Saul's family comes out at me. His name is Shimei son of Gera, and he curses me in his Benjamite accent as he comes out.

He pelts me and all my officials with stones, even though the troops and the special guards are on my right and left.

Shimei spits at me, and says, "Get out, get out, you murderer, you scoundrel! The Lord has repaid you for all the blood you shed in the household of Saul, in whose place you have reigned!"

I do not bother to wipe my face. I figure I deserve whatever comes my way. Living in the palace I have been shielded for many years from talking with common folk, with the single exception of hearing them when presiding over legal disputes. Which is why I am surprised to learn, at this point, that there are people who hold a grudge against me, people who may have been hurt by things I have done years back, to make my reign stable. For me, this is an education.

The last thing I want to do is engage with Shimei, because it may only cause him to double down on his insults. So the only thing I say is not aimed at him at all.

"Save me from all my transgressions," I pray. *"Do not make me the scorn of fools."*

Shimei says, "The Lord has given the kingdom into the hands of your son, Absalom."

At hearing this Abishai, son of my sister Zeruiah, who is walking right next to me, is stunned. He says to me, with his usual fervor, "Why should this dead dog curse my lord the king?"

And Shimei says, with a reddened face, "Damn you! Who are you calling dead dog? I'm very much alive!"

To which Abishai says, "Not for much longer!"

And I say, "Oh, stop it."

And Abishai grits his teeth. "Let me go over," he says, "and cut off his head."

But I tell him, "My son, my own flesh and blood, is trying to kill me. How, then, can you blame this Benjamite?"

"But," he stammers, "but, but—"

"Leave him alone," say I. "Let him curse. He is but an instrument to give me what I deserve. Perhaps the Lord will look upon my misery and restore to me his blessing instead of his curse today."

Meanwhile, Shimei goes on. "Get out, get out!" he cries. "You've come to ruin! And you know why? Because you're a murderer!"

You may think that I am a saint for not answering back, and that my silence in the face of my accuser comes easy to me. Nothing is farther from the truth.

I said, I will watch my ways, and keep my tongue from sin.
I will put a muzzle on my mouth, while in the presence of the
wicked

So I remained utterly silent, not even saying anything good.
But my anguish increased, my heart grew hot within me.

We go on along the road while Shimei is going along the hill side opposite us, cussing as he goes and casting stones at me and showering me with dirt. I close my eyes. It is at times like this that I miss my lyre the most. It allows me to forget everything in the world, except the music, the tender music of my pain.

On I go, and under my breath I begin to sing.

But I am a worm and not a man
Scorned by everyone, despised by the people
All who see me mock me.
They hurl insults, shaking their heads.

*

I miss my son, in a way I have never missed him before, knowing that he is not, and never will be, the man I expected him to become. The kiss I never got from him must be rejected, it must be held back by distance, which I must increase, because if I ever face him again, one of us will die.

I have expected his forces to arrive already, but they are not here yet. Now that we have mules to carry us, our escape is somewhat faster. Still I continue to worry that it is not fast enough. And so, on and on we go, under the cover of darkness, with barely any sleep.

At midnight we arrive at the Jordan river. We walk along its bank, and hours later catch a first glimpse of something magical: a haze rises there, over the Sea of Galilee, lifting away the edge of gloom. The glassy surface turns the landscape of the opposite shore upside down, and makes the glimmering of stars twinkle in the water.

In the distance, boats of fishermen seem to float over the deep blue. This is a tranquil, dreamy sight, one that invites us to a much needed rest. It lulls me into a sense of security, which I suspect is false.

The women are exhausted. They beg me to stop and let them wash their clothes. Bathsheba whispers in my ear that she knows a secluded place somewhere along the river bank, where she might bathe later, and why not join her there when everyone else falls asleep.

But I tell her, "I wish we could stop, but it's almost daybreak."

And she says, "If we were to continue, which way would you go?"

And I say, "I don't know."

I want to tell her that I am too tired to think, but by the tender look in her eyes she already knows it, and feels for me.

So instead I say, "I wish we can stay on this side of the river, and continue north around the Sea of Galilee. But then," I tell her, "when Absalom catches up to us, we may find ourselves with our backs to it, with no rafts to carry us over to the other side."

"Then," says Bathsheba, "why not cross the Jordan river right now, where it's narrow, before we reach the Sea of Galilee? Why not go around it, on its opposite side?"

"Because," say I, "none of us speaks the languages of the people who live beyond, east of the river. Here, at least, the land belongs to us, and we belong to the land. There, we'll be foreigners in a foreign land."

Just then I hear a sudden din, a commotion coming from the back of the procession, and two young people with crumpled, muddied clothes are brought before me. Their feet are red with blood. Their faces are caked with dust. Their lips are dry, cracked. It takes me a while to recognize them.

These are Ahimaaz, son of Zadok, and Jonathan, son of Abiathar. They must have been running here all the way from Jerusalem, with some urgent news to tell me.

I order Abishai to draw some water from the river so they may wash their feet, clean their faces, and wet their lips. He offers them a drink as well, but they push it away.

In a breathless voice Jonathan cries, "Set out and cross the river at once!"

And Ahimaaz croaks, "Your previous advisor, Ahithophel, has devised a plan against you!"

"Don't spend the night at the fords in the wilderness!"

"If you stay here, you and all the people with you will be swallowed up!"

I don't ask questions. There is no time for that, not now. I know—we all do—that we must bolt out of here, because if these messengers have managed to find us, so can the enemy.

I mean, so can my son.

So I order my troops to build a makeshift bridge over the river, and help everyone cross it to the other side. By daybreak, no one is left who has not crossed it. Which is when the bridge is taken apart, and its parts smashed, and later discarded some distance away from the river, so the enemy will have to work harder to reconstruct it.

Only then do I go back to the two young men, Ahimaaz and Jonathan, to hear the full details of what they wish to tell me. By now they have rested their feet. Still, the expression on their faces is rather tense.

"Your majesty," says Ahimaaz, "we were staying at En Rogel, which is a place just outside the City of David, and—"

"Is that what they call it, still?" I ask.

"No," says Jonathan. "It's called City of Absalom, since yesterday."

And Ahimaaz says, "Never mind what they call it, we couldn't risk being seen within its walls."

"Nor could we risk visiting our fathers, the priests, because their homes were surrounded by spies."

"So," I wonder out loud, "how did your fathers manage to inform you what's going on in the city?"

"A maidservant was to go between them and us, to give us the latest news," says Ahimaaz. "But a spy saw her talking with us, and he told Absalom, which is why we had to leave home in a hurry."

Seeing that his friend is running out of breath Jonathan continues in his place. He says, "We went to the house of a woman in Bahurim, who had a well in her courtyard. We climbed down into it, and from down below we saw her spread a covering over the opening of the well. In a blink, darkness fell upon us, but we could hear a pinging sound, and knew she was scattering grain over the covering, to obscure our hiding place."

"Then, all of a sudden, a noise, a great clamor!" cries Ahimaaz. "Swords clanking, boots marching by the side of the well. We heard the door swinging on its hinges as the woman came out of her house. We heard soldiers asking, 'Where are they?" and the woman asking, "Who?" and them shouting, 'You know who!" and her claiming, "I wish I knew! Who are we talking about, exactly?" and them bellowing, "Don't pretend you don't! Where are they, the two scoundrels? You hiding them?' Finally, in place of answering, she asked, 'See that brook, over there? I think I saw them crossing it, in that direction!'"

"We couldn't believe our luck, as the boots marched away," says Jonathan. "The soldiers must have searched all over that brook, and even beyond it, only to return to Jerusalem empty handed."

I tell them, "I'm glad you're here, safe."

"So are we," says Jonathan.

"And now," says Ahimaaz, "Let us tell you the important thing. We have news, which is why we had to come here, in the first place."

They are eager to tell me what happened—but before they can start, another messenger appears at the edge of the camp.

I tell him to wait his turn.

So Jonathan says, "Your confidant, Hushai the Arkite, came to see our fathers, Zadok and Abiathar, the priests. He told them what happened in the palace."

"I'm listening," say I.

"As you may know your son and the men of Israel came to Jerusalem, and Ahithophel, your previous adviser, was with him. Then your confidant, Hushai, went to Absalom and bowing to the ground he praised him, and proclaimed, 'Long live the king! Long live the king!'"

I smile. "Oh, he's good!"

"Indeed he is! But at first Absalom narrowed his eyes, and out of suspicion he tested him, he said, 'So this is the love you show your friend? If he's your friend, why didn't you go with him?' To which Hushai said, "No, your majesty! The one chosen by the Lord, by these people, and by all the men of Israel—his I'll be, and with him I'll remain. Furthermore, should I not serve the son? Just as I served your father, so I'll serve you.'"

I slap my knees, unable to stop laughing. "Oh, he's better than good!"

"Then Absalom, who was quite spent after the performance he gave at the expense of your concubines, gave a huge yawn and stretched his arms this way and that, and asked, 'Well, what now?' And Ahithophel stepped forward, and suggested, 'I would choose twelve thousand men and set out tonight in pursuit of David. I would attack him while he's weary. I would strike him with terror, and then all the people with him will flee. I would strike down only the king and bring all the people back to you. The death of the man you seek will mean the return of all.'"

At that I tense up.

Jonathan goes on to say, "Perhaps Absalom was sleepy, or simply too lazy to organize his forces, and so he sought an alternative advice."

"Which he got," says Ahimaaz, "from your confidant, who told him, 'The advice Ahithophel has given is not good this time. You know your father and his men. They're fighters, and as fierce as a wild bear robbed of her cubs. Besides, your father is an experienced fighter. He won't spend the night with the troops. Even now, he's hidden in a cave or some other place. So I advise you: Take the time to organize! Get all Israel, from Dan to Beersheba—as numerous as the sand on the seashore—be gathered to you, with you yourself leading them into battle. Then we'll attack him wherever he may be found, and we'll fall on him as dew settles on the ground. Neither he nor any of his men will be left alive. If he withdraws into a city, then all Israel will bring ropes to that city, and we'll drag it down to the valley until not so much as a pebble is left."

"And that," I ask, "was the advice my son accepted?"

"It was."

I shake my head in amazement. "Really? According to that, the size of an army is better than its speed, and preparation better than action! I could've told him a thing or two about surviving in the wilderness with my gang, as a young fugitive. Despite being a small gang, we could wreak havoc on Saul's army any given day!"

"I suppose," says Jonathan, "that Hushai talked for such a long time, and added so many details, and shed such glory, or the illusion of it, over everything he said, that there was no stopping his speech—unless, of course, you agreed with him."

"Which Absalom did," says Ahimaaz, "because above all he wanted to go to bed already, and turn off the lights."

"And after that," says Jonathan, "he moved rather swiftly, not to lay his hands on you, my lord, but to tuck himself under the blankets, where he would be visited by visions of grandeur in the days ahead."

Ahimaaz concludes the story by saying, "Everyone around him nodded their head, and clapped their hands and praised his strategy, and agreed with him that the advice of Hushai the Arkite was better than that of Ahithophel. Which is why they're still asleep, all the men of Israel, dreaming of being valiant and heading here for the attack."

"Which is why," say I, "we will survive."

Now I turn to the other messenger, who has been standing at a distance, waiting to speak to me.

I demand, "What news d'you bring?"

And he says, "Good news, your majesty! It's about Ahitophel, your previous advisor."

"I've always admired him for his wits. The advice he gives is like that of one who inquires of God."

"Yes, my lord. That's what everyone says."

"So what is it now? Has he stopped supporting my son? Has he defected?" I ask, hearing the eagerness in my voice. "Is he coming back to serve me?"

"Well, no," says the messenger. "When he saw that his advice hadn't been followed, he saddled his donkey and set out for his house in his hometown. He put his house in order, burned some of his own notes, wrote a will, signed it, and then, then he hanged himself."

At hearing this I feel—oh, I wish I knew how to put words to it—I feel as if the wind had suddenly gone out of me. I feel choked, as if I were the one to be discovered, dangling there from the ceiling.

I figure that with his exceptional wit Ahitophel must have foreseen something what is still unclear to me: the ruin of the conspiracy, if I am allowed time. He knew that upon its failure, one thing is sure to follow: his punishment at my hands. In his pride he decided to deny me control of his destiny, and being an ill-tempered man, he kicked the chair from under him.

I do not wish to think anymore, nor do I wish to imagine my adviser swaying there, back and forth, on the loop of the rope, with his neck fractured, and his eye looking down upon his signature.

I turn and walk away from everyone, and climb up towards the peak of a nearby hill, overlooking a blazing sunset over the Sea of Galilee. This is a new angle for me, because in the past I saw it only from our parts, looking eastwards. Now, looking in the opposite direction, I am stunned at this view, this revelation. A red sun is hanging upon its reflection in the red waters.

All along the shore, an intricate net of lagoons, bays, springs, and waterfalls is sprawling as far as the eye can see. With every step, lush foliage wraps around my feet. Underneath I feel broken branches, tortuous roots, and stems that have started to rot in the shadow of all that greenery.

I pick up a branch and lean upon it for the last stretch of my climb. When I get to the top I use the tip of it to write into the earth:

Do not fret because of those who are evil
Or be envious of those who do wrong
For like the grass they will soon wither,
Like green plants they will soon die away.

Absalom, My Son, My Son

Chapter 14

Lacking provisions, and unprepared for the icy winds in the north, we walk as one, huddled closely together, until we arrive a week later at Mahanaim. This is a fortified town near the Jabbok river, which feeds its water to the Jordan river. The stronghold is protected not only by the manmade walls around it but also by natural boundaries, such as the flow of the river, and the slopes of its valley. Throughout history it was known as the perfect site to serve as a sanctuary for important fugitives.

Nearly three decades ago, when I became king over my own tribe and had to fight against the rest of them, I made a mental note to myself: if I would ever become a fugitive, this would be my first place of refuge. At the time I told myself, Stop thinking like a wanted criminal! You are a king now, are you not? What are the chances of having to run for your life?

That was then. This is now.

Problem is, natural boundaries are a nice thing, but withstanding an attack upon us in this place is going to require a lot more than that. I need my first in command, Joav, son of my sister Zeruriah, to help me train the troops. Rarely, if ever, have they practiced defensive warfare. In fact, even their offensive skills have turned rusty, because such is the effect of peace. It makes things dull.

Right now there is too much turmoil, so I need him. Oddly, he seems to have disappeared without a trace. I assume that my nephew is alive. Why? Because as a feared man, his death would have been celebrated throughout the land—in spite of the numerous victories he won, in my name, on the battlefield.

To my amazement there is no news about him, not even rumors, and no one is certain as to his whereabouts. Where ever he may be I know what he must be thinking. "Let the boys play before us!"

No, I must correct that. "Let the old man and his boy wrestle with each other, until one of them remains standing. For now, the best course of action is to sit on the sidelines and watch them spill each other's blood."

Alas, such is his loyalty!

If I am defeated, he will find it shamelessly easy to join Absalom and offer his services to him as his first in command. After all, the two of them have a blood tie in common: they are cousins. What is more, they are of the same generation. Even though I am not fifty yet, to them I am a has-been.

Above all, nothing is more useful to a new king than being protected by someone certifiably ruthless.

I may have lost Joav—but gained new supporters. One of them is Barzillai the Gileadite, an elderly man with the drive of a young one. He lives near Mahanaim, in a place called Rogelim. From there he has brought us bedding, bowls, and articles of pottery. Amazingly, his generosity does not end there.

He is willing to provide us with all our needs, now and in the future.

He bows before me, which is not an easy thing to do, not only because he is eighty years old but also because he is carrying sacks of wheat and barley on his back, while pointing the way to his son, Kimham, and to all his servants, so they may know where to place the bags of flour, roasted grain, beans and lentils, and jars of honey, curds, and cheese for all of us to eat.

"Your majesty," he says, "these are for your people, as they have become tired, hungry, and thirsty in the wilderness."

With a quick, efficient manner Barzillai arranges these provisions inside this storage place and another in the stronghold. Then he casts a shrewd look at me and asks, "When is your first in command coming here?"

I shrug. "God knows!"

"Want to know what I think?"

"I think you think what I think."

For some time, we stand there in silence.

Then he says, "I'm told that in the past Joav won favor with your son, by paving the way for him to come back to Jerusalem, after his long exile."

"Just so," say I. "And then, then Absalom chose to express his gratitude in a strange manner. He burned Joav's field."

"I suppose," says Barzillai, "that it was his way to show your first in command that between the two of them, he is the one more ruthless."

I say, "To this day Joav hates him for that, which means that he fears his cruelty. Truly, he respects it. As a result of the fire, he begged me to open my arms to the arsonist. I mean, to Absalom."

And Barzillai says, with worry in his voice, "If Joav does show up, keep a distance from him."

To which I say, "I always do."

"I'm told he's good with knives."

"The best."

"And he likes to strike his victim under the fifth rib."

"It's his favorite spot."

"You know," says Barzillai, "he may be looking for a way to bring the revolt to its conclusion."

At that I gasp. "You mean, assassinate me?"

"Beware," he says. "For him, the end justifies the means. He'll reap the reward from your son's hand."

I shake my head. "No, that's too wild!"

"Is it?"

"We're family, all three of us."

"Eh," he says. "The family you have is worse than total strangers."

"That happens to be true," I admit. "I find it so easy to make friends with new people, such as yourself."

"No wonder," he says. "There's no guilt, no blame, no raw emotions boiling under the surface."

Again, we say nothing. There is nothing to be said, when the truth is clear to both of us. The family I have is the reason my life is in danger.

After a while he asks, "You know the meaning of the name of our town, Mahanaim?"

"I do," say I. "It means, *Two camps*. This is where Jacob, the legendary patriarch of our nation, divided his retinue into two camps, and cowered in the back of the second one, for fear that his brother Esav would attack him."

"So," says Barzillai, "this is perfect place for you! It celebrates what families are all about!"

My crown has become a hollow symbol, as I have become the king of nowhere. With this territory comes the danger of assassination. Mahanaim is known also for that.

Less than three decades ago, it was here that Abner, the Benjamite general, set Ish-Bosheth son of Saul on the throne and crowned him king over the tribes of Israel. When his general was stabbed to death by my first in command, the puppet king went limp in the absence of his puppeteer. Then, two of his own men concluded that this was the time to get rid of him.

Having had enough of his lack of action, they figured that his days are numbered anyway, and the best thing for them would be to hurry up ahead of others who may get the same brilliant idea, and cut off his head.

Lack of action, I conclude, was a mistake for the son of Saul, and so it is now for me. I should have punished my firstborn, Amnon, for raping Tamar. I should have punished my second son, Absalom, for murdering Amnon. I should have stamped out this revolt at the first signs of unrest, instead of looking the other way. To achieve stability in my family and around the land, my response should have been as severe and as swift as these crimes.

*

Lately, finding solitude is difficult, because I have no palace, and no chamber to separate myself from the world. Instead, the Jabbok river has become my relief, my hiding place, not only from my enemies but also from my friends.

Its headwaters rise from a spring named by the locals *Gazelle spring*. Thickets of poplar plants and salt cedars grow abundantly along its banks, and higher up, on the hillsides— forests of wild oak. Immersing myself in the stream, and listening to the way it babbles over me, I find myself inspired.

Deep calls to deep, in the roar of your waterfalls.
All your waves and breakers have swept over me.

At the horizon I spot a small mountain, called Mount Mizar, in the shadow of the more spectacular, snowcapped Mount Hermon, which is glowing majestically in the morning sun. Together they form two links, as if they were of the same family: a child and a parent.

I try not to think about my son, but in spite of myself the words come, and the longing follows.

My soul is downcast within me.
Therefore I will remember you
From the land of the Jordan
The heights of Hermon
From Mount Mizar.

*

My spy tells me there is bad news and good news.

I tell him, "Start with the bad news."

And he says, "The bad news is that Absalom is getting closer. He's crossed the Jordan river, with all the men of Israel. They're already camped in the land of Gilead."

"I can't wait for the good news."

"The good news is that he's appointed Amasa over the army."

I know Amasa. He may have been chosen as a new military man for a new era—but he comes from the same place as Joav: my family. He is the son of Jether, an Ishmaelite who married Abigail, the daughter of Nahash and the sister of Zeruiah, the mother of Joav. If this seems complicated to you, imagine how I feel, having to contend with such convoluted relations! The thing to keep in mind is this: we are all one family. Amasa is the nephew of Joav, who in turn is my nephew.

"The good news," says the spy, thinking, perhaps, that I have not listened to him, "is that Amasa is now in charge of organizing his army."

"It's better than a sharp stick in the eye," I tell the spy. "But how is that good news?"

"Because," he replies, "it means that Joav has missed his moment of opportunity with Absalom, and will not serve as his first in command."

Thinking I heard a footstep behind me, I look over my shoulder, and who should be standing there, but the man that has mysteriously gone missing for over a week: Joav! He is smiling slyly under his mustache. In a moment he will come over and pat me fondly on the shoulder as if he has never left me.

"You!" I say.

And he says, "What?"

And I demand, "Where were you?"

And he says, "I had to do something which I rarely do."

"What's that?"

"Thinking."

"Was it painful?"

"Ha! Was it ever!"

"And?" I ask. "Did you arrive at any conclusions, having gone through this unfamiliar process?"

"I did," he says. "I figured out what you want to know."

"Which is what?"

"Who'll come out of this fight alive."

"Really?" I blurt out. "You know the name of the victor?"

He smirks. "Maybe I do!"

"You think I'm going to ask you?"

"Why shouldn't you?"

"Because," say I, "you'll simply lie to me, won't you?"

He answers by asking, "Why should I?"

"For no better reason than to flatter me. I know you want your job back."

"I do, your majesty. So even if you don't ask, I'll tell you."

Our eyes meet. He holds my gaze for a long time.

At last, "The victor," says Joav, "will be the one who can hang on longer."

"That's it? That's all you're going to tell me?"

"What more d'you want?"

"You know," say I, waving my hand at him, "I've been thinking too."

He holds himself back from asking, What about.

So I tell him, "I'm thinking that from now on I must divide control of the military."

"Ha! What's new about that?" he asks, without inviting an answer. "Both of us know that you've always thought this way."

"But today, Joav, I'm going to do it."

I muster the men and appoint commanders of thousands and commanders of hundreds. I send out the troops, a third under Joav, a third under his brother, Abishai, and a third under the Philistine general, Ittai the Gittite.

Joav marches ahead of the other two commanders, shaking his head. Clearly, he is unwilling to share military power. He narrows his eyes looking at them, and tightens his grip on the hilt of his sword.

His brother, Abishai, keeps a distance from him, and so does Ittai, because everyone knows that when Joav comes too close, as if to hug you or whisper a dirty joke in your ear, the next thing you know is a stab under the fifth rib.

To prove that I am serious about the new military hierarchy I must proceed to the battleground at the head of all three. This is something I am reluctant to do, not only because I find no joy in slaughter and not only because I have always detested what wearing an armor forces you to become—but also because I fear that I will have to cross swords with my son, Absalom.

I fear that I will die. Worse, I fear that I will kill him.

Even so I tell the men, "I myself will surely march out with you."

As if they can read my mind, they say, "You mustn't go out!"

"I mustn't?"

"If we're forced to flee, the enemy won't care about us. Even if half of us die, they won't care. But you are worth ten thousand of us. It would be better now for you to give us support from the city."

What choice do I have but to agree with them? "I'll do whatever seems best to you," I say.

My boys, Solomon and Adonijah, beg me to let them march out with everyone else, because up to now they have been playing with toy swords, and because to them, war seems like a fun game. The last thing I want is to give Absalom a chance to eliminate his brothers. So I tell them to stay with their mothers, because who else will stay behind to protect them?

Then I stand beside the gate while all my men file out in units of hundreds and of thousands. I give a nod to each one of them as they pass by me, because they are risking their lives for my sake, and because—oddly enough—they see it as a privilege.

I am touched by their loyalty, and worry about them as if they were my own sons, the way sons ought to be. If we suffer defeat, some of them may come back on a stretcher. Others may be left behind to rot on the battlefield.

Having been to so many wars in the past, I cannot help but imagine the soundless spread of wings, as birds of prey hover in the air, as they descend upon lifeless figures and peck at their wounds. I hear groans of pain even as I watch these young, fresh faces, many of whom are smiling at me, waving farewell.

All of them hear me loud and clear when I bellow, "Halt! One more thing, before you go!"

Joav, Abishai and Ittai stop marching, and all the men behind them come to attention. The last thing they expect of me, as they head for a crucial battle, is a plea for restraint.

"Be gentle with the young man Absalom," I tell them, "for my sake."

*

My army marches out of the city towards the forest of Ephraim. From here it looks like a lovely green patch rolling over the hills east of the river. The canopies of its trees swallow up noise, such as the cries of war, which must be earsplitting at a closer range. Yet all I detect, sitting back here in Mahanaim, is an eerie silence. I hear nothing, and no one hears me as I chant:

> *Those who want to kill me set their traps*
> *Those who would harm me talk of my ruin*
> *All day long they scheme and lie.*

All day long I wait. I get up from my seat, dust it off, and sit down again. At noon my friend, Barzillai, brings me bread and water, but I am too anxious to eat or drink.

An hour later the air starts cooling down, which forces me to find a patch of sunlight to keep myself warm. The shadows keep rotating around me, so I must adjust the placement of my chair, setting it first outside the outer gate, then inside the inner gate. Above me, the watchman has gone up to the roof of the gateway by the city wall. I see his feet dangling overhead.

By evening he calls out to me.

I stop biting my nails, long enough to ask, "What is it?"

And he reports, "I see a man running alone."

"Good, this is good, truly it is," say I. "It's not the entire army, fleeing before the enemy. You sure he's alone?"

"That's how it seems. Yes, alone he is!"

"If so, he's bringing good news. I'm sure of it!"

By now I, too, see the runner. To put it more precisely I catch sight of his shadow, separating from the edge of the wood. Now and again it disappears completely from sight, as he goes into a lush dale.

"He's coming," the watchman assures me.

"Where is he?" I ask, heart pounding. "I don't see him."

"He's closer and closer," says the watchman. Then he points farther ahead and cries, "And look, look out there, your majesty!"

"What is it? What now?"

"A second man, running alone!"

To which I say, "He must be bringing good news, too."

Then the watchman says, "I think I know the first one. He seems to run like Ahimaaz son of Zadok."

"He's a good man," say I. "For sure, he comes with good news."

By now I, too, recognize the way he runs, which seems skewed, because one of his heels is still swollen from his previous journey. Ahimaaz calls out to me, "All's well!"

And the watchman cries out, "Is it?"

Upon arriving here Ahimaaz tries to answer, but instead he huffs and puffs, trying to catch his breath. He bows down before me with his face to the ground, and unable to speak he resorts to clapping his hand together, with great glee.

At last he manages to utter, "The news is good!"

"I knew it!" I say, patting his back. "News from a good man can't be bad, can it?"

At last he takes a deep breath, and says, "Praise be to the Lord! He has delivered up those who lifted their hands against my lord the king."

"What does that mean?" I ask. "Is the young man Absalom safe?"

I hear the anxiety in my voice, and so does Ahimaaz. He stops talking, and when he opens his mouth again he gasps, only to stumble over his words. "I saw confusion, great confusion, your majesty, just as Joav was about to send the king's servant and me, your servant, but I don't know, I really don't know for sure what it was."

"Stand aside," I tell him, "and wait here."

So he steps aside. I hear him speaking excitedly with the watchman, telling him the details of the battle, about which I have neglected to inquire.

"We won! We won!" he says. "The enemy was defeated by our men, and the casualties today were great—twenty thousand men!"

In amazement, the watchman asks, "Really? How did that happen?"

"We know the terrain," says Ahimaaz. "Most of them don't. The battle spread out over the whole countryside, and the forest swallowed up more men today than the sword."

"Are they coming back to attack us?"

"No! The revolt has been crushed for good, and the remainder of the men of Israel have fled to their homes."

Meanwhile, the second runner arrives, a dark skinned young men with an Egyptian accent.

"My lord the king," the Cushite calls out, "hear me, hear the good news! The Lord has vindicated you today by delivering you from the hand of all who rose up against you."

To his surprise, and mine as well, I care nothing about how the battle developed, and how victory was achieved. Instead, all I want to know is one thing, and one thing only. "Is the young man Absalom safe?"

The Cushite raises his hand, and with a cruel glint in his eye and a slicing gesture across his throat, he starts laughing. Perhaps he hopes to sweep me into his bloodthirsty joy.

I cover my eyes so as not to see him, but I cannot stop myself from hearing his voice, saying, "May the enemies of my lord the king and all who rise up to harm you be like that young man."

At that, I am badly shaken.

I go up to the room over the gateway and close the door behind me, and clap a hand over my mouth, clap it tightly to stop myself from uttering these gruff sounds, these sobs.

This is not the first time I find myself in the presence of death. I mourned for friends and for enemies, and managed to shape my feelings into the most eloquent eulogies, articulating the meaning of grief for large audiences. I knew they needed to wash themselves of sorrow, by devoting a moment to remember the departed, and vow to keep him in their thoughts forever, before allowing him to be forgotten.

I used to enjoy expressing myself, even in sadness. Yet now, the only cries that come bursting out of me are so violent, so forceful, that they are nearly devoid of language.

"Oh my son Absalom! My son, my son Absalom!"

I thrust my crown across the floor till it clangs, clangs, clangs. And to that sound I collapse into the corner, and press my lips like a lover against the stone wall, letting its coldness seep into me.

"If only I had died instead of you! Oh Absalom, my son, my son!"

*

I have no idea how much time has passed since I closed myself in this place. From time to time the door starts screeching on its hinges, as someone comes in. He brings in food, which I know because the plate rattles against the surface of the floor, before his footfalls fade away. Whoever he is I grant him nothing, not even as much as a glance, and I leave the food untouched.

Yet even as I want to be left alone, I find myself dreading my loneliness.

> *My heart pounds, my strength fails me.*
> *Even the light has gone from my eyes.*

My friends and companions avoid me because of my wounds.
My neighbors stay far away.

Then, somehow, I know that it is morning. I hear my troops coming back, passing through the inner and outer gate, directly below this room. Some are moaning because of their wounds. Others are laughing, happy to be alive. Many of them ask why I am not out there to congratulate them for such an unexpected triumph.

Someone, perhaps the gate keeper, must be pressing a finger to his lips to hush them, because at once they lower their voices. And I know that for the whole army, the victory this day is turned into mourning, because of me. They steal into the city this day as men steal in who are ashamed when they flee from battle.

I can block loud talk, but whispers have a way of penetrating me. I wish I could forget words. I do not want to hear what happened. Let someone else listen. Let someone else write about it.

The Sacrifice

Chapter 15

The battle has been decided, which seems to make people relax back into their routines. Trusting that peace will follow, they come out of their hiding places and start traveling the land. Even my old scribe, Nathan, has arrived here from Jerusalem. I hear him outside, interviewing soldiers in his sheepish manner, which puts them at ease and lets them tell their story.

Bleating at them, "Tell me," he says, "what happened, exactly, in the forest of Ephraim?"

I hear the soldiers chuckling around him and imitating his manner of speaking over and over, so as to refine their impression of him till it becomes accurate enough to fool the ear.

But one of them asks, "You sure you want to know?"

"Yes," says Nathan. "I do."

"Absalom," says the soldier, "crossed my path in the woods. I saw him turning and riding in the other direction on his mule, and as the mule went under the thick branches of a large oak, his hair got caught in the tree. He was left hanging in midair, while the mule he was riding kept on going."

"Now, this may be a silly question," says Nathan. "He had a weapon on him, did he not?"

"Yes. A sword."

"So, why didn't he use it? Why didn't he cut himself loose?"

"That," says the soldier, "is a mystery to me, too."

And after a long pause, he adds, "Perhaps Absalom was hoping that someone would bring his mule back and position it there, right under him, and climb up to separate his lovely hair, strand by strand, from each one of the twigs on the bough of that tree."

"Did he cry out for his men, so they may come to his help?"

"Of course not! He was afraid that our men would hear him. So he bit his lips, and suffered the pain, and waited. And the longer he waited, the more his hair got tangled, over and under the limbs of that tree."

"And still, he wouldn't raise a hand to free himself?"

"No! I think he loved his hair too much and wished to keep it intact."

The scribe is silent for a moment. Then, "You're right," he says. "Absalom would cut it only once a year. To my astonishment, he used to make a big show of it."

"Admired by many," says the soldier, "it was only himself that he loved."

"Going back to what you witnessed out there in the forest," says Nathan. "What an unusual sight that must have been!"

"Oh, it was terrifying!" cries the soldier. "And yet, Absalom looked more magnificent than ever! He was beginning to look like a tree himself, with his hair pulling at its roots, branching out, twisting every which way in that light, that dim light that slipped here and there through the leaves, dappling him."

Nathan utters a sigh, which is immediately echoed by the soldiers around him.

Meanwhile, the soldier goes on to say, "Then I called Joav. I told him, 'I just saw Absalom hanging in an oak tree.' And Joav cried out, 'What! You saw him? Why didn't you strike him to the ground right there?'"

"And? What did you say to that?"

"At first, nothing. So he said, 'Ha! If you had killed him I'd have had to give you ten shekels of silver and a warrior's belt.' To which I said, 'Even if a thousand shekels were weighed out into my hands I wouldn't lay a hand on the king's son.' Joav glanced at me shrewdly, as if to ask, 'Why not?' So I responded by asking, 'Don't you remember? As we headed out of town for this battle, the king made a point of asking you and everyone else, for his sake, to be gentle with the young man Absalom.'"

"Even so, weren't you tempted?" asks the old scribe. "I mean, it's not every day that a soldier gets a chance to win ten shekels of silver and a warrior's belt!"

"For that I had to put my life in jeopardy," says the soldier, "because nothing's hidden from the king."

"Come now, how would he find out?"

"To remove blame from himself, Joav would've pointed me out to him. Ignoring the fact that Joav gave me a direct order, he would've accused me of slaying Absalom."

"So," says the scribe, "When Joav saw that you wouldn't do what he asked of you, what did he do then?"

"He shrugged, saying, 'I'm not going to wait like this for you.' Then he rode out to the oak tree, from which Absalom was dangling."

"And when he got there, what happened?"

"Joav raised his eyes to the king's son, who shuddered to see him, and asked, 'Why should I spare you? Give me one good reason to do so!' And Absalom said, in a husky voice, pleading for his life, 'Because we're family!' To which Joav said, 'Ha! I thought so too, until the day you dared touch what's mine and burn it!' And he took three javelins in his hand and plunged them into Absalom's heart while he was still alive in the oak tree."

Nathan asks nothing more. Instead he mutters, "Oh lord."

But the soldier presses on. "The body was still writhing in great pain, and blood was squirting down, forming a puddle beneath it, which darkened the ground."

"Wasn't Joav afraid of the king's wrath, for disobeying his orders to spare the life of his son?"

"Joav prepared himself for it. He called ten of his armor-bearers, and told them to surround Absalom and strike him, so that he died by many hands."

"How fitting," says Nathan.

And the soldier wonders aloud, "How so?"

"History repeats itself. Joav ordered the execution the same way Absalom had ordered the execution of his half brother, Amnon, so that the blame wouldn't fall on a single person, even if he was the one to order it."

After a long silence, the soldier says, "And then, Joav sounded the trumpet and at once, the troops stopped pursuing the enemy, because both armies knew that it was over."

"I've seen many of the bodies, which were brought back to town," says Nathan. "Where's Absalom's?"

"The armor-bearers took it," says the soldier. "I saw them throwing him into a big pit in the forest, after which they piled up a large heap of rocks over him."

"I don't suppose he got a eulogy, did he?"

"Not exactly. The only words said were Joav's. He wiped his hands of dust, slapping them soundly against each other, and spit over the burial place, after which he said, 'You should've known, Absalom, what I told your father. I always expected that the victor in this fight would be the one who could hang on longer.'"

*

I press my hands over my ears, to dull the sounds around me. And in that silence, the only voice that plays in my mind is that of my father, who died two decades ago.

I remember: when I was a child he used to tell me old legends, one of which I found particularly terrifying. He said, "Abraham, the patriarch of our nation, bound his son, Isaac, to an altar, in preparation for the sacrifice."

In my fright I raised my eyes to him and asked, "Why? Should a father sacrifice his son?"

And he said, "I think it was just a test of faith."

And I said, "Such a test is meant for flunking!"

"Perhaps you're right," he said, chuckling. "Which is why the angel of God stopped Abraham at the last minute, and told him to withhold his knife."

My father hugged me, so I could feel the closeness between us, and in his low, melodic voice whispered something in my ear. It was a quote from that odd legend, the conclusion of which was supposed to quell my fears.

"And Abraham lifted up his eyes," he whispered, *"and looked, and behold: behind him, a ram was caught in the thicket by his horns. And Abraham went and took the ram, and offered him up for a burnt offering in the stead of his son."*

Now, all these years later, I am thinking about that ram, caught in the thicket. I cannot help but seeing a vision of my son in him. Caught in the oak tree, there he hangs, frozen forever in that minute, the last minute of his life, waiting for his sacrifice. I imagine him lowering his eyes to me, which breaks my heart, as I see the dread in them, the utter helplessness. And yet, like him, I cannot move, cannot lift my hand to cut him loose. I stand there trembling, praying for a some miracle, but no angel comes to his rescue to stop the javelins from being hurled at him. There they are, plunging into his heart.

In childhood as in old age, my question remains unanswered. Should a father sacrifice his son?

I am so tired, so burdened by guilt.

Of one thing I have no doubt: my men are not at fault. As a leader, the responsibility for what they have done is truly mine. Was it not the wish to save my life that drove them to take his?

I lost my son not because of his affront to me, but because of my own absence, my failure to be there myself, to protect him.

With his death, what kind of a father am I?

*

In a voice that is older than my father's I whisper to myself.

I am bowed down and brought very low
All day long I go about mourning.

I am lying there hours, perhaps even days, facing the wall, trying to drift away from myself into a dream, into an invented memory of a distant, carefree past. Then, a noise. I hear the door creaking, and heavy boots squeaking one, two, three steps, till coming to a stop directly behind my back.

"Get up," says a voice, gruffly.

For a moment I find myself mute. I have not spoken at all lately, which seems to affect my throat, my lips, my tongue. To my surprise, they are slow to produce sounds. In a listless, sluggish manner, "Let me be," I manage to utter, somehow.

"That," says Joav, "I can't do."

I prop myself up against the wall—but keep my eyes averted, so as not to see the man who killed my son and not to attack him.

He asks, "Why can't you look at me?"

"You're the last man I want to see."

"Ha! You think I care what you want?"

"Obviously you don't," I say. "Brazenly have you proven it, by daring to disobey me!"

"What I've done is for your own good, and you know it."

"What does that mean, when you've killed a part of me?"

"Enough!" he bellows. "I've had it! I can't stand all this moaning and groaning and tearing your clothes to shreds! It shows weakness, which is something I abhor. Get up, get up right now, and clean yourself!"

"Go away," say I. "Who're you to tell me what to do?"

"I could say I'm family," he says, coldly. "But between us, that matters little to me."

"You need more than a blood tie to be considered family."

"Consider this: what I care about is power. I won't let you loosen your hold on it, because by doing so you also loosen mine."

"What you talk about is greed," say I. "Which is why my son is dead."

"Dead he is," says Joav. "Consider yourself lucky!"

And aside he mutters, "Ha! What a scoundrel, what an insolent boy! Good riddance!"

I get up on my feet and weak as I am, I try pushing him out the door. "You," I grunt. "Out!"

He swings it wide open, puts a hand around my waist, which is when I realize that I have lost a lot of weight since my escape from Jerusalem. Then he forces me to go out with him.

"Look," he says, pointing out at the crowd, which starts gathering down there to watch us. "All these eyes sparkling, all these young faces, waiting to see you."

"What are they waiting for? I'm not the man they want."

"In their eyes you're more than a king. They think of you as their father."

"Who wants a father such as me?"

Joav casts a look at me out of those steel gray eyes.

"Today," he says, harshly, "you've humiliated all your men, who have just saved your life and the lives of your sons and daughters and the lives of your wives and concubines."

I hate to admit that he is right, so I say nothing in return.

"You love those who hate you," he says, "and hate those who love you. You've made it clear today that the commanders and their men mean nothing to you. You would be pleased if Absalom were alive today and all of us were dead."

I shake my head. "No," I mumble. "That's not what I meant to do."

Joav claps his hand on my shoulder. "Now go out," he says, "and encourage your men."

I stand there, at the top of the staircase, nearing the edge.

"I swear by the Lord," he says, "that if you don't go out, not a single man will be left with you by nightfall. This will be worse for you than all the calamities that have come upon you from your youth till now."

I go down the stairs and take my seat in the gateway. My men start coming before me, bowing to the ground to pay me honor. They hang their heads between their shoulders, afraid, perhaps, of what I might tell them about the killing of Absalom, unsure how to express condolences.

I recall how they passed here on their way to the battleground. I nodded to each and every one of them, which I do once again. There are fewer of them now.

I thank them for bringing about such a decisive victory. Yet looking at the procession of the wounded I find it hard to distinguish what I see before me from defeat.

What I spot in their eyes is pain and worry—but more than that, love. This is when I know that they need me, and something awakens in my heart, something that has no name, yet.

I try to guess at it. Perhaps, fatherhood.

Return to the City of David

Chapter 16

Excitement starts building up amongst my followers. They are looking forward to the journey back home, which is going to coincide with the traditional pilgrimage to the City of David at springtime. For their sake I set my grief aside, because it is private, and make plans for a successful return, which is a challenge, given the confusion and the continuing unrest in the country.

Having left my royal robes in Jerusalem I carry no marks of distinction. Few of the locals in the villages outside Mahanaim care to give me another look. To them I seem nearly transparent, like any other old, homeless man, which to my surprise affords me a certain freedom. Walking in rags from one village after another I get to hear what they say. Without having to send my spies around, I realize that throughout the tribes of Israel, people are squabbling.

One says, "The king has delivered us from the hand of our enemies. He's the one who rescued us from the hand of the Philistines. He's our hero! Why did we ever join the revolt against him?"

And another asks, "But where is he now?"

"God knows!"

"He's fled the country to escape from his son. And Absalom, whom we anointed to rule over us, has died in battle. What will become of us? No one is ruling the land!"

"So why d'you say nothing about bringing the king back?"

"Aren't you listening? I'm not saying nothing! I'm definitely saying something, which is this: bring him back!"

"Yes!" says the first one. "Let him rule over us, as he did before!"

At hearing this I decide to write a letter to Zadok and Abiathar, the priests: "Ask the elders of Judah, 'Why should you be the last to bring the king back to his palace, since what is being said throughout Israel has reached the king at his quarters?"

Before sealing it I add the powerful *flesh and blood* argument —even though I am cautious of certain members of my extended family and the danger they have posed to my life by joining the revolt.

I avoid mentioning that in these troubled times, we should all be cautious of each other. Instead I write, "You are my relatives, my own flesh and blood. So why should you be the last to bring back the king?'"

The priests write back, "Done!"

"Done?" I ask. "What does that mean?"

And they reply, "We've delivered the message to the elders."

"Well?"

"No word from them yet."

While awaiting a response and talking myself into being patient I consider my new, three-pronged military hierarchy. Within a day it seems to have crumbled, because two of the commanders—my nephew, Abishai, and the Philistine general, Ittai the Gittite—defer to the third one, Joav, who is most ruthless of them all.

With a mixture of awe and fear, they shrink away from him, and no wonder! He is full of swagger as he boasts loudly, in front of everyone, including me, about squashing the revolt singlehandedly, and executing my son.

As a result, everyone starts to call him my first in command again. So I figure I must find another candidate for the job. To my delight, a new name comes to mind: Joav's nephew, Amasa, who was in charge of the forces of the revolt as my son's first in command. Given his defeat, his military leadership skills are questionable, and his experience—lacking. Even so I wish I could convince him to replace Joav.

By an odd contradiction I believe that a weak-minded first in command may end up strengthening my rule, because he might actually obey what I tell him.

I think I might use *flesh and blood* argument once again, in my new letter to Zadok and Abiathar. I write, "Say to Amasa, 'Are you not my own flesh and blood? May God deal with me, be it ever so severely, if you are not the commander of my army for life in place of Joav.'"

And they reply, "Done!"

"What does that mean?"

"We've delivered the message to him."

"Well?"

"No word from him yet."

*

The first tribe to accept me back as their ruler is my own. The women of Judea love me, which I already know—but now I win over the hearts of the men, so that now they are all of one mind.

The elders send word to me, "Return, you and all your men."

So I lead my men as far as the Jordan. On the opposite bank is a place called Gilgal, which is known in our history for forging a bond between our tribes. It was here that Joshua, the leader who succeeded our legendary Moses, ordered the Israelites to take twelve stones from the river, one for each tribe, and place them there, to celebrate crossing it into the land of Canaan.

And it is beyond that circle of stones that I spot two large groups of people, awaiting to greet me: on the right, a group comprised of the men of Judah, and on the left—a group of Benjamite men, well known for keeping a grudge against me, because I was serving the Philistines while my predecessor, Saul, was fighting his last battle against them. To this day, they wish to resurrect his dynasty.

These Benjemites are lead by none other than Shimei son of Gera, the man who cursed me with such remarkable enthusiasm, chased me out of my own city, and spat on me only a few days ago, when I fell from power.

At seeing him I brace myself, thinking that his presence here must mean trouble, because clearly, there is nothing better he enjoys than throwing mud, stones, and vile expressions at me. Shimei hurries down with the rest of the men who are crossing the ford to escort me back. To my surprise, he outdoes everyone else, hailing me at the top of his voice and bouncing about like a lame grasshopper. Feigning the most joyful of joys, he comes forward, cheering me loudly.

When he comes near, Shimei falls prostrate before me and cries, "May my lord not hold me guilty!"

And I say, "Why not?"

His buggy eyes nearly pop out of his head. "I beg you," he grovels before me. "Please, your majesty, please don't remember how your servant did wrong on the day my lord the king left Jerusalem."

"I didn't just leave. I was chased out!"

"May the king put it out of his mind."

I shrug, "Why should I?"

"Because," he squeaks, "your servant knows that I've sinned."

"You know it, and so do I!"

It is said that a drowning man will clutch at straws, but what Shimei clutches, to my dismay, is my hand. "But, but today," he stutters, "today I'm here as the first from the tribes of Joseph to come down and meet my lord the king."

"As far as you know I'm the same man now as I was then," say I. "Nothing changed, except for my luck. How sad it is that when I fell from power, you spit on me with such deep, intense hate—"

"There's nothing deep about my feelings. I'm a shallow man."

"So now that I've risen, how shallow is your sudden devotion to me?"

Shimei can find nothing to say. Beads of sweat are glistening on his upper lip as he leans to kiss my hand.

I pull it back. "Enough!" I tell him. "Stop slobbering over me!"

Then my nephew, Abishai, claps a hand over his shoulder and asks me, "Shouldn't he be put to death for this? He cursed the Lord's anointed!"

His eyes are bloodshot, which reminds me of his brother, Joav. These men have been fighting in my service too long. Trained for aggression, they mistake it for a solution for every problem.

I say, "What does this have to do with you, you sons of Zeruiah? What right do you have to interfere?"

"Time and time again we risk our lives for you," says Abishai. "Our brother, Asahel, died on the battlefield."

"I loved your brother," say I, simply. "But you, you made his death a cause for more violence, more unrest between our tribes."

"His death, by the hand of a Benjamite, was brutal," he says, "and brutally we had to avenge it."

"This," say I, "is a day for peace."

"Even so," he says, pointing at Shimei, "this Benjamite should be punished!"

"Should anyone be put to death in Israel today? Don't you know that today I am king over the entire land? This," I say, "is a day for unity."

Finding his voice again, Shimei wails, "Please, your majesty, please have mercy on me!"

And I give him my word, I say, "I will spare your life."

Yet in my gut I know that a day will come when this man and others like him will pose a danger to the throne. Today the country is celebrating my return, and joy should not be mixed with sorrow. I will not put him to death—but in the future, when one of my sons succeeds me, he will.

Heaving a sigh of relief Shimei collapses at my feet, and just to make sure, he asks, "Promise?"

"Yes," say I. "Promise."

Meanwhile Barzillai the Gileadite, the man who provided for us during our stay in Mahanaim, is coming down with his son Kimham to cross the Jordan with us, before it is time to say farewell.

Barzillai is old, eighty years of age, but there is always a youthful glint in his eyes. Now that we have embraced for the last time, they sparkle with tears.

I tell him, "Cross over with me and come stay with me in my palace. I'll provide for you, as you have done for me, now and in the future."

But Barzillai shakes his head. "How many more years will I live," he asks, "that I should go up to Jerusalem with the king?"

I answer by asking, "Can we see what the future may bring? Who can say how long either one of us shall live? Come with me to my city, where I can spoil you with every pleasure, every luxury you may imagine."

"Eh," he says, smiling. "I'm now eighty years old. You think I can tell the difference between what's enjoyable and what's not? Can your servant taste what he eats and drinks? Can I still hear the voices of male and female singers? Why should your servant be an added burden to my lord the king?"

"What burden?" I ask. "For me, your company is a delight! Betrayed by those closest to me I've despaired of the possibility of friendship. Your company makes me believe in it all over again."

"Eh, it's too late for me," he says. "Your servant will cross over the Jordan with the king for a short distance, but why should the king reward me in this way?"

"You really want me to tell you why?"

"Why shouldn't you?"

"Don't you know?" say I. "You're like a brother to me."

"Let me return, that I may die in my own town near the tomb of my father and mother. But here," he points at his son, "is your servant Kimham. He is a part of me, that I wish to leave in your hands. Being young, he's eager to leave his old man and look for adventure. Let him cross over with my lord the king, and go with you wherever you go."

"Kimham will cross over with me, and I shall treat him as if he were my own son, only better," I promise. "And as for you, anything you desire from me I'll do for you."

"My only desire," he says, "is to know you're back in Jerusalem, safely."

By now all the people have crossed the Jordan. It is time for me to go. I kiss Barzillai and we part ways. By the time I turn to look back, all I see is a distant figure fading into the lush landscape of the eastern bank. My heart is heavy as I wave farewell. Here I am, a king in rags, heading into a land torn asunder.

*

When I was still living in the palace, ensconced in the illusion of safety, I had no idea that the union between our tribes is less that stable. Forced out into the open, I realize now that the divisions between them are deeper than deep, which was why they have found the revolt so terribly appealing.

Even now, some people are eager to start a new rebellion. A troublemaker named Sheba son of Bikri, a Benjamite, sounds the trumpet and shouts, "We have no share in David, and no part in Jesse's son! Every man to his tent, Israel!"

So all the men of Israel desert me to follow him. The crowds have thinned. When I arrive at the City of David a week later I find myself surrounded by only a handful of men, all of whom belong to my own tribe, the tribe of Judah. I have hoped that my return would look triumphant—but no longer does it resemble a parade, let alone a pilgrimage. Alas, it looks even more miserable than my escape.

I call my newly appointed first in command, Amasa, to come before me to get his orders. When he finally arrives, he seems too sleepy to focus on what I tell him.

I say, "Summon the men of Judah to come to me within three days, and be here yourself."

"What, your majesty?"

"What d'you mean, *What*? Are you hard of hearing?"

"Sorry," he yawns. "I've never talked to a king before."

"Never mind talking, what I need from you is action."

"Oh," he says, "I'm really good at that, trust me!"

"Really?" say I. "I wasn't too impressed with whatever it was that your forces managed to achieve in the forest of Efraim."

He gives me a heavy-eyed look, and says, sluggishly, "Oh, what my forces managed to achieve was defeat, which means that I can only do better in my next mission."

"And your next mission, d'you know what that is?"

"No. Sorry, I wasn't listening."

So I repeat, stressing each and every word so it may sink, somehow, into his brain. I say, "Summon the men of Judah to come to me within three days, and be here yourself. Can you do that?"

And he says, "I think I can," before letting another yawn escape from his mouth, which tells me that quite possibly, he is not as driven to succeed as I have hoped him to be.

I wait and wait for his return, to no avail, and when a few days have passed without as much as a message from him, I figure that he must have failed on his mission, or else fallen sound asleep on his way there.

So what choice do I have but to place my trust elsewhere? At first I consider Joav for the mission, but decide to keep him out of it. Instead I say to Abishai, his brother, "Now Sheba son of Bikri will do us more harm than Absalom did. Take Joav's men and pursue him, or he'll find fortified cities and escape from us."

Abishai is quick to organize. I watch him as he takes Joav's men, and the Philistine mercenaries, and all the mighty warriors, and starts marching ahead of them out of Jerusalem, in pursuit of Sheba son of Bikri. Then, just before they disappear into the hills, I spot the one man I was hoping to keep out of this mission, and away from a position of power in my army.

There he is, my former first in command, Joav, walking alongside his brother, wearing a military tunic, over which a belt is strapped, with a dagger in its sheath. At once I send a spy to follow him, because I must learn what he is up to. His uninvited presence is sure to end up in one calamity or another.

*

When my spy comes back he bows before me and gives me the one line I have hoped never to hear again.

He says, "There is good news and bad news."

And I say, "Start with the bad news."

So then he tells me, "While Abishai and his forces arrived at the great rock in Gibeon, Amasa came to meet them."

Few places have an air of mystery as much as Gibeon, because of its monumental, rock-cut architecture, which inspires you to think of the possibility of man cradling himself in the womb of nature.

Alas, this is only an illusion. It was there, at the pool of Gibeon, that Abner, the Benjamite commander, suggested to my first in command, Joav, "Let the boys play before us," which resulted in the death of Asahel, Joav's brother, and in a fierce civil war between our tribes.

I was hoping this was ancient history.

"Your majesty?" says the spy. "Did you hear me? I said, Amasa came to meet them."

"What?" I cry. "A bit of social chitchat is fine, when you have nothing else to do! How come he has time for that, at the expense of doing what I asked of him? What a nincompoop!"

"That, my majesty, is just the right word for him."

"Amasa should be right here, right now, to report to me!"

The spy shrugs. "I don't think you'll be hearing from him any time soon."

I demand, "What does that mean?"

"It means that your nephew, Joav, was only too happy to meet him. As he stepped forward, his dagger dropped out of its sheath. He smiled, in a way that was utterly transparent to me, and to everyone else—except, perhaps, Amasa. I knew what it meant: Joav was going to be patient. He has waited this long. He could wait as long as it took for Amasa to drop his guard."

"I think I know where this is going. But knowing Joav, and knowing how much he hated Amasa for taking a job that in his mind, belonged only to him, I suppose he was not going to wait too long."

"Indeed," says the spy. "He said to Amasa, 'How are you, my brother?' and took him by the beard with his right hand, as if to draw him into a kiss. Amasa was too surprised to resist him. Before he could utter a single word, Joav lifted his dagger with his left hand, which was unexpected by his victim, and plunged it into his belly. Amasa fell, and his intestines spilled out onto the ground. Without being stabbed again, he died."

I utter a deep sigh, knowing that this crime will have to go unpunished. I have no choice now but to restore Joav to his position as my first in command—not only because he is the only one ruthless enough to perform the necessary tasks, but also because I cannot keep him out of office, as he'll go on killing my candidates, one after another.

Meanwhile, the spy presses on.

"Amasa," he tells me, "lay wallowing in his blood in the middle of the road. Everyone who came up to where his body was crumpled in a pool of blood stopped. To make sure they keep on going, one of the men dragged him from the road into a field and threw a garment over him. After Amasa had been removed from the road, everyone went on with Joav to pursue Sheba son of Bikri."

At hearing this I gasp, as a memory comes to mind. I recall, word for word, what I learned about the earlier incident: the death of Asahel, Joav's brother, who was slain there years ago, at pool of Gibeon. Word for word I whisper:

So Abner thrust the butt of his spear into Asahel's stomach, and the spear came out through his back. He fell there and died on the spot.
It was such a horrific sight to behold that every man stopped when he came to the place where Asahel had fallen and died.
But his brothers, Joav and Abishai, continued to pursue Abner,

"History repeats itself," I mutter. "And so does violence."

"Shall I go on?" asks the spy.

"Oh, of course! I can't wait for the good news," I say. "And I hope it's not as bloody."

"It's bloodier."

"Tell me about it."

The spy takes a deep gulp of air, so it can last him for an entire story. "So," he says, "after he killed his nephew, Joav joined his brother Abishai, and both of them pursued Sheba son of Bikri, who had arrived at the city of Abel Beth Maakah. Our troops came and besieged him there. While they were battering the wall to bring it down, a woman called from the city, and asked to speak with the first in command. 'We are the peaceful and faithful in Israel,' she said. 'You're trying to destroy a city that is a mother in Israel. Why d'you want to swallow us up?' 'Ha! Far be it from me!' Joav replied, 'I have no appetite for swallowing you or your city. All I want is to get my hands on a man named Sheba, who has lifted up his hand against the king, against David. Hand him over, and I'll withdraw from the city.' To which she said, 'His head will be thrown to you from the wall.'"

"And so it was?"

"So it was," confirms the spy. "The woman convinced the men who stood around her to save their city by cutting off the head of Sheba son of Bikri. They threw it to Joav, and he caught it in one hand while raising the trumpet to his lips with the other. At the sound of it, his men dispersed from the city."

*

Once the last rebellion has been quelled I go back to my palace, which is something I have postponed until now, because of my desire to reach out to my people, sense what they are thinking, and share in their hardships without being separated from them by walls. This is one lesson I have learned from my journey: you can hear a lot by just listening, which you can do better when you have no diplomats, historians, and servants to alter the story, so it might feel more soothing to you than it really is.

For a king, there are advantages to being homeless.

The first sign that the palace was looted is the way the gate to the courtyard is sighing in the wind, swaying lopsided back and forth, forth and back on a single hinge. The doors of the palace carry muddy boot marks, and the latch is broken. I enter, and find myself appalled at the sight of destruction.

The geometrical design of the mosaic floor, which has been laid out in my court with such care and artistry, is missing most of its details. Here and there, its stones—including the colored glass from Tyre, the shells from the delta of the Nile, and the pebbles from the river Tigris—are missing.

As for the curtains, they are crumpled in a heap, torn and utterly soiled. In the women's quarters, the frames of the embroidered panels are smashed. Pearly beads are strewn across the floor, the only remnant of the jewelry that was stolen. The rooftop outside my chamber has been torched, and charred slats that used to be part of the wooden lattice around it are now dangling over the edge.

But the most heart-wrenching sight is not the damage to my property—but to the women, the ten concubines whom I left behind, on the night of my escape. They are wandering listlessly about the place, looking more dead than alive. If anyone comes near them, they start screaming in fright.

The elders tell me that these women are tainted. They belong not to me, but to the man who has forced himself upon them in my absence. My son, Absalom, possesses them from beyond the grave, so I should treat them as if they were his widows.

They are kept in confinement, which inevitably brings my daughter, Tamar, to mind. She is still living alone in Absalom's house, a desolate woman.

Jerusalem itself seems desolate. I remember writing about it, "The city has no history yet. Erected log by log, with cedar trees imported from Lebanon, and slab by slab, cut out of the hardest rocks in the Judea mountain range, it will become my mark, my political statement. It will stand for hope."

In the City of David, history is marked by the ruins of its houses, the scars of its fighters, the graves of its children, and the silence of its women.

I invite my young sons, Adoniah and Solomon, to ride with me to the Kidron valley. I would like them to sit with me awhile in the shadow of that pillar, which Absalom has erected as a monument to himself during his lifetime. It would do me good to think about the dead while embracing the living.

Adoniah declines, giving me some lame excuse about having to go to some party.

Solomon, too, is busy. He says, "I can't! Not now, father."

I look at him, wondering how it is that a young man who has just turned twenty still looks like a kid. He still has freckles on his nose, and does not know what to do with his scrawny arms, except let them hang by his sides.

I ask, "Why not?"

"Perhaps tomorrow," he says at last.

So I say, "Come with me! Whatever it is, can't it wait?"

And he says, "No, not really. I must compose a new beginning for my book, which I'll call the *Song of Songs*."

"Again a new beginning? What's wrong with the old one?"

"It went up in smoke," he says. "When we escaped from Jerusalem I forgot to take my scrolls with me. They've been burned to smithereens. Smithereens," he adds, "is a word I like."

I say, "Why can't you write it later, when we're back?"

"Because," he says, "the words are still fresh in my mind, more or less. If I wait, they'll go away, and I'll be left with nothing. Nothing but smithereens."

And I say, "Then, invent new words!"

"I'm no writer," he says.

"Then, why toil on a book?"

"I collect things. The most valuable of them are words and expressions, especially those I hear from my mom and you. Nothing I may invent will ever compare to, '*Do not arouse or awaken love until it so desires.*'"

"D'you understand it now?"

He shakes his head, till the ghost spots of his freckles dance in the air around him.

"Well?" I ask. "Do you?"

"No," he says. "I don't really want to understand. There is a certain mystery in the words, which I adore. Why should I tear it apart by reason?"

In the end I ride to the valley of Kidron by myself. On the way to Absalom's monument I hang my head down. I count the rhythm of my horse, galloping. I look at the soil. It is moist and fertile. Years ago it was brought here, to my gardens, from the hills, the faraway hills near the conquered city of Rabbah. It looked foreign then, in its dark color, but now it seems like part of the land. Time, I tell myself, has a way of healing all wounds.

Glancing over the edge of the ravine I see, through the fragrant pollen that fills the air, a lone oak tree. It looks different now, perhaps because I have come back from a long journey to discover it anew. Its roots, and the dry brush that used to surround it, are covered by flowers, new flowers that were not there before. When I come closer I see that they are opening their petals as if to let out a blood-red flame.

It is spring.

I spot a silhouette out there, at the edge of the royal garden, where it falls into the ravine. Whether real or imagined, there she stands, my daughter Tamar, amidst the bloom: a dark figure with a slender, long shadow flitting over the edge.

I close my eyes and try to imagine her coming forward, closer to me. A smile sparkles in her eyes, and it is over that light that I see, in an altogether different layer, my son, Absalom, hanging by his hair from the limbs of another oak tree, in the faraway forest of Efraim.

What have I done, causing one calamity to follow another? Sin followed by assault, followed by execution, followed by revolt, escape, execution, revolt...

Lord, do not rebuke me in your anger
or discipline me in your wrath.
Your arrows have pierced me,
and your hand has come down on me.
Because of your wrath there is no health in my body;
there is no soundness in my bones because of my sin.
My guilt has overwhelmed me
like a burden too heavy to bear.
My wounds fester and are loathsome
because of my sinful folly

When will this end? How can I break it, for my sake, for my children, and for this land?

Epilogue

I adore the way she calls my name, the way she sighs. With every sweet word I fall deeper into her eyes. To save myself I close them. Somewhere inside I pray, *"Do not remember the sins of my youth, and my rebellious ways. According to your love remember me."*

Bathsheba must sense that I have regained consciousness, because she cries, "David?"

And behind her, Abishag echoes, "David?"

I open my eyes, only to realize that I am in my chamber. The scroll, which Bathsheba has given to me, hoping I would read it in time, lays discarded in the shadow, down in the corner. At this point I know what must be written upon it, even without reading. If I let Adoniah succeed me, he will eliminate the other contenders for the throne. Her life and the life of her son, Solomon, are both in grave danger.

I smile at both women, which must be a frightening sight, because the next thing I know Abishag has fainted. There she is, by the foot of the bed, lying utterly motionless.

Bathsheba acts with her usual swiftness. She pours the entire jug of water on the girl, which revives her. With a stupefied expression Abishag gets up from the floor and gathers one of the blankets around her naked body, not before she finds time to blush.

Bathsheba opens the chamber door to let her out. Then she comes back and takes her seat upon the bed, by my side. I am surprised to realize that she clings to me.

"What is it you want? What's troubling you, and what is your request?" I ask her, with the singsong tone of our usual game. "Be it as much as half the kingdom I shall give it to you!"

"You know," says Bathsheba, "One of these days I will say yes to that."

"Why shouldn't you?"

"You mean, right now?"

"If not now, when?"

"My lord," she says, "you yourself swore to me your servant by the Lord your God: 'Solomon your son shall be king after me, and he will sit on my throne.'"

"I never promised you that," say I. "It's a nice try, though!"

"Maybe you did and maybe you didn't," she says, with a shrug. "I don't think you remember."

"Why shouldn't I? I remember everything!"

"Do you? Perhaps you imagine most of it!"

"Without imagination," say I, "how would I have a vision for the future?"

"How about taking stock of the present, first and foremost?" she asks. "Now your son, Adonijah, has become king, and you, my lord the king, don't even know about it!"

At that, my jaw drops.

"He has?" I cry. "Really?"

"He's sacrificed great numbers of cattle, fattened calves, and sheep, and has invited all the king's sons, Abiathar the priest and your first in command, Joav. In short, he's invited everyone but your servant, Solomon."

I am about to shake my fist, and invent all kinds of names for Adonijah and for his offensive behavior, especially because he has not bothered to ask for my blessing, when Bathsheba lays a hand on my arm to arrest it. Then she says, in a voice that is as quiet as it is serious, "Don't. Shaking your fist is of less importance than using your wisdom. This is a crucial time."

"Don't I know it!"

"My lord the king, the eyes of all Israel are on you, to learn from you who'll sit on the throne of my lord the king after him. If you don't act now, then as soon as my lord the king is laid to rest with his ancestors, I and my son Solomon will be treated as criminals."

While she is still speaking Nathan the prophet arrives. He bows with his face to the ground, which is a good thing, because the sight of his pointy goat beard has always irked me, as has his bleating.

In his roundabout way, he asks, "Have you, my lord the king, declared that your son, Adonijah shall be king after you, and that he'll sit on your throne?"

"How can you even suggest that?" I cry.

"I'm not suggesting, I'm just saying."

"Of course I haven't!"

Seeing how annoyed I am Bathsheba bows to me in parting and out to the corridor she goes.

Meanwhile Nathan clicks his tongue.

"Today," he reports, "Adonijah has gone down and sacrificed great numbers of cattle, fattened calves, and sheep. He's invited all the king's sons, the commanders of the army and Abiathar the priest. Right now they're eating and drinking with him and saying, 'Long live King Adonijah!'"

"The scoundrel!"

"Is this something my lord the king has done without letting his servants know who should sit on the throne of my lord the king after him?"

At that I pound my fist against the mattress, which is not as impressive as I hoped it would be, because you can barely hear a thud. "I've heard enough!" I tell him. "Bring Bathsheba back, right now!"

At once she comes back from behind the door, which tells me not only that she has been listening to every word but also that these two have, most likely, timed their appearances before me. They must have collaborated to make their stories fit so perfectly together. Even so I trust what they say, because I know that for each one of them my decision is going to be a matter of life and death.

Bathsheba kneels before me.

I peer into her eyes and at the top of my voice, I vow, "As surely as the Lord lives, who has delivered me out of every trouble, I'll surely carry out this very day what I swore to you by the Lord, the God of Israel"

"Which is what?"

"Which is this: Solomon, your son, shall be king after me, and he'll sit on my throne in my place."

I have expected her to utter a sigh of relief or express gratitude by way of kissing me, but instead she says, "I knew you'd remember! Didn't I tell you that you made me a promise?"

"Somehow," I say with a chuckle, "it's all coming back to me."

To which she smiles. "May my lord King David live forever!"

Behind her Nathan says, "Long live the king," but at this point I am unsure if he means me or my son, Solomon.

After that I arrange for Zadok the priest, Nathan the prophet and my bodyguard, Benaiah, to accompany Solomon down to Gihon, which is a place of marvel in the Kidron valley. I charge my mercenaries, the Kerethites and the Pelethites, with guarding him. Thank God for these Philistines! If not for them, there would be no secure way to anoint my son, my chosen one, king over Israel.

Given the support of our tribes, which is shaky at best, such is the way to ensure my dynasty.

"When you arrive there, blow the trumpet," I instruct the priest.

"I will," says the priest, "with all my might."

"And shout," I tell the prophet, "'Long live King Solomon!'"

He replies, "I will, your majesty, with everything I have in me."

"Then," I tell Benaiah, "you are to go back up to the palace with Solomon, and he is to come and sit on my throne and reign in my place. I've appointed him ruler over Israel and Judah."

"Amen!" says the bodyguard. "May the Lord, the God of my lord the king, so declare it!"

All three of them clap their hands, as it is such fun to plot against Adonijah's plot.

"As the Lord was with my lord the king," says Benaiah, "so may He be with Solomon to make his throne even greater than the throne of my lord King David!"

I have a sudden urge to cry, "Not so fast! I'm still here, am I not?" but somehow I control it and let it go unsaid. I mean, what good will it do?

*

And so Zadok the priest, Nathan the prophet, and my bodyguard, Benaiah, hurry out of my chamber together, to escort Solomon to Gihon. I have chosen this spring, whose name means *gushing forth*, for a reason.

It flows three to five times daily in winter, twice daily in summer, and only once daily in autumn. No one has ever gone through the passage all the way to its outlet, which is hidden in a cave. It is deep enough to preserve a sense of mystery about it.

Despite being intermittent, the spring is a reliable source of water for the Pool of Siloam, located in the Kidron valley, which stores up water for the City of David. It made settlement possible here—not only for drinking water but also for irrigation of the royal gardens. Since ancient times, it has been considered a source of sustenance. What better place to ensure an orderly transition of power for my dynasty, and what better symbol for the future!

All my attendants have followed Solomon on his journey, so here I am, left all alone in my chamber. There is not much to do but follow my son from afar, in my own way.

I imagine the priest taking the flask of oil from the sacred tent to anoint him. There is a flash of gold in the air as he starts pouring, which brings to mind the fragrance of oil. I smell it as if it were dripping over my own head.

Somehow the days of my youth, when Samuel the Prophet arrived at my father's house to choose the next king of the land, come rushing back to me. I close my eyes and take in a deep breath, in which I detect a dash of powdered bark, a pinch of scented medicinal leaves, sweet cinnamon, calamus and cassia, mixed together into olive oil according to an age old formula passed down the generations.

By now, I imagine, the sound of trumpet must be reverberating back and forth between the walls of the valley. Soon the trilling of pipes will be heard, along with the thud of footfalls in various rhythms of dancing, and laughter, resounding laughter of men and women rejoicing.

I can almost hear them shouting, and find myself startled by the words, in which my name has been omitted to mark an irreversible change.

"Long live King Solomon!"

And the last thing I imagine before sleep comes is Adonijah, pressing his hands over his ears to stop it, stop hearing the blaring of the trumpet, while his guests are rising in alarm, just about to disperse.

*

I awaken from my dreams when Solomon comes in. Here he is, standing over me. It must be very late or else very early, because the chamber is dark, so dark that even his freckles cannot be spotted.

I try to sit up in bed, but find myself humiliated by my frailty, as I cannot do it. Instead I raise my hand in greeting, and at once he places his inside mine, as if he were not a young man but a little child, craving warmth.

"Dad," he says, "are you cold?"

"Not anymore," I say, and mean it. At long last I feel connected to a son of mine.

My son leans over and for a brief moment, lays his face upon my chest.

"I need you," he says, simply. "Don't leave me."

To which I say, more to myself than to anyone else, "I'm about to go the way of all the earth."

Solomon says nothing, but his hand trembles in mine.

"Be strong," I say, "and act like a man."

"It's not easy."

"Don't I know it."

"But," he says, "on second thought I think I can *act* like a man, even as I'm learning to be strong."

I smile, but my heart aches to know that having been anointed, a change will soon come over him. He will soon sense it himself. The poet in him must stand aside and make way for a leader to be born.

How can I prepare him for that? I have so much advice in me, which I am not sure he would learn to accept. There is so little time! I fear I may stumble over my words in my attempt to teach him. So I take a deep, labored breath and tell him, "To mete out justice, you must harden."

And he asks, somewhat reluctantly, "Must I?"

"Yes," say I. "I've reigned forty years over Israel: seven years in Hebron and thirty-three in Jerusalem. It's time for you to sit on my throne. Let your rule be firmly established."

Cutting in, "I have a feeling," he says.

"What kind of a feeling?"

"You're going to give me a lot of advice, aren't you?"

"It's now that I must give it."

"Not sure I'm ready for it, dad."

"You yourself know what Joav, son of Zeruiah, did to me," I say and immediately cut myself off, because I cannot talk about the death of Absalom, not now. Perhaps, not ever.

So I start again. I say, "Joav supports your brother, Adonijah, and will always scheme against you."

"That I understand," says Solomon. "He'll be a danger to me even if he serves me."

"You know what he did to two commanders of Israel's armies, Abner son of Ner, and Amasa son of Jether."

"I do."

"He killed them," say I, "shedding their blood in peacetime as if in battle, and with that blood he stained the belt around his waist and the sandals on his feet."

I feel a shudder going through my child.

"Deal with him," I advise, "according to your wisdom."

Solomon raises an eyebrow. "So you won't tell me what to do with him?"

"No," say I. "You're the king now, are you not? Just remember this: don't let his gray head go down to the grave in peace."

To my surprise, "Wait," says the kid. "Let me write this down, so I can figure it out later."

"This is not a quote for your *Song of Songs*," say I. "You must understand it now, or it's going to be too late for you."

Just then I recall what my first in command, Joav, said to me a long time ago. "One day, you'll want me dead," he said. "When that day comes I would run in there, to the Tabernacle, to seek asylum. I would take hold of the horn, the brass horn in the corner of the altar. Without it there would be no place for someone like me to escape your judgment."

I debate with myself if I should express that which to me seems obvious: Joav should be executed without fail, even if he takes refuge in the holiest of places. I want to give Solomon my advice—but decide against it. I must trust him to come to the right conclusion on his own.

For me, letting go is the hardest thing.

I am tempted to give him a slight hint—a quote, perhaps, from one of my better known psalms—so he understands that the tent of God should not provide shelter to someone as ruthless as my first in command.

So in spite of my failing voice I sing these words to my son, hoping they will guide him, somehow, in the future.

> *Lord, who may dwell in your sacred tent?*
> *Who may live on your holy mountain?*
> *The one whose walk is blameless,*
> *Who does what is righteous*

Solomon rocks slightly with the melody, but says nothing, not a word.

I look at him as if to ask, Well? Do you understand?

His eyes are fluttering around, as if to refuse me, refuse what he knows he must do. I meet his gaze and hold it. I hold it for a long time, until something inside me hammers one, two, three heartbeats.

Which is when he says, "I do, father."

"One more thing."

"It's not more advice, is it?"

"Why shouldn't it be?"

"Because," he says, "It's simply too much."

Over his objection, "Remember," I tell him, "you have with you Shimei son of Gera, who called down bitter curses on me the day I went to Mahanaim. When he came down to meet me at the Jordan I promised not to punish him. But now, don't consider him innocent! You're a man of wisdom. You'll know what to do to him."

"Bring his gray head down to the grave in blood?"

"Exactly," I say. "Evil men are to be cast aside like thorns, which are not gathered with the hand. Whoever touches thorns uses a tool of iron or the shaft of a spear. They're burned up where they lie."

"Dad," says Solomon. "I never heard you talking like that."

"Like what?"

"Like a farmer."

"What I am," say I, proudly, "is a shepherd."

"Yes. That's what you are," he says, and his voice fills, suddenly, with a sense of admiration. "There will never be another one in history like you, father, I'm sure of it: the commoner who became king."

"Now, one more thing."

"Not another gray head to be brought down, is it?"

"No."

"What then?"

"It's about my dear friend, Barzillai of Gilead. Show kindness to his son and let him be among those who eat at your table."

"I will, father."

"He stood by me when I fled from my enemy."

"From whom?"

"Your brother, Absalom."

Just then, an odd thing happens to me. The minute I say that name, which I have not uttered since my return to Jerusalem, something stirs in me. I do not even know what to call it. It wells up, it floods, it permeates all of me: a reverence for life, for every precious moment of it, the good and the bad. I wish I could go back and live every twist, every turn of my story all over again. With the greatest of lusts I savor both joy and pain.

"Solomon," I whisper.

"Yes, father," he says. "I'm here."

"Today," I say, "is a perfect day."

He turns his head away, perhaps to spare me from seeing that his face is awash with tears.

Then, glancing blankly at the window, "It is," he says. "It's a perfect morning." To which he adds, unexpectedly, "I love you."

"Help me," I say. "Take me out to the roof. I want to see the sun rising over my city one last time."

*

The doors of my chamber open before me. Supported by my son I labor one step after another, till I make my way out. This is like no sunrise I have ever seen before. A sphere of fire, in which I spot innumerable flames of orange, red, and purple, rolls over the dark hills, setting their outline ablaze.

Below, somewhere in the women's quarters, children are starting to awaken. I hear their voices: some cry, others call for their mothers. One of them, a young girl, runs out to the courtyard, then stops and turns her head back.

I squint against the light, which allows me to recognize her: she is my grandchild, Absalom's child.

Now she waves at me. Her laughter is so pure, so melodic. It is full of silvery notes, which reminds me of my own daughter, Tamar, and the way she used to laugh, before silence overtook her.

I want to go down to the child and put my arms around her to keep her safe, now and in the future—but I know that it is not in my power. Even so I murmur to her, across the distance, "Let you never surrender to silence, because if you do, it would leave you with the rusty, poisonous taste of shame."

The child has opened the gate. Like me, she is watching the sunrise. I wonder what it means for her. Perhaps, hope.

One day my daughter, Tamar, will stop listening to the dictates of those who wished to hush her. She will no longer obey the words, 'Shut up,' which she must still be hearing in her mind, in the voice of Amnon, who raped her. Nor will she obey the words, "Be silent for now," in the voice of Absalom, who sought to protect her.

The real shame—now I know—is to consent to silence. A day will come when she will transform her suffering into meaning, into words.

There is no motion anywhere, except for the clouds. They are rolling in, hanging full and heavy over the hills of Jerusalem, roaming over me like an upside down flock of sheep.

It is then that a memory comes back, the shining memory of distant days, when I was watching over my father's herd. From where I stand now, my childhood seems carefree—until I remember how resentful I felt that first time when he told me that the next day I would be left with the sheep all by myself. They were taller than me, which frightened me. I was full of disdain and wished I could rebel.

But I did not, because what choice did I have? We lived faraway from the lowlands, where you could farm the land. A shepherd I had to become, so I pretended to know my way. I walked ahead and to my surprise, the herd followed. In that rugged, mountainous terrain, finding new areas for grazing kept me on the move, farther and farther away from Bethlehem, even as my longing for my father grew stronger. I imagined coming back to him at the end of the day.

When wind raged around me I would whisper words into it. When it died down I would hum a melody. In my loneliness I would listen to the echoes rolling back from the hills, singing with me.

Even though I walk
Through the darkest valley

I will fear no evil
For you are with me.
Your rod and your staff
They comfort me.

For me, this is farewell. A sadness is descending upon me, and something else, too: a yearning to forgive and be forgiven. It hammers inside me, one, two, three heartbeats.

I close my eyes and there is my father, opening his arms to me. At long last I am ready to let go of my pride and submit to his will. Here I am, coming home.

And in that last heartbeat I am happy.

~ The End ~

About this Book

David loves his sons. The last thing he expects is that they will topple him from the throne. Who among them will remain by his side? Who will be not only loyal, but also eager to continue his legacy?

For now, David remains silent, even as Amnon rapes Tamar, even as Absalom lures Amnon to his death. In families other than his, such crimes may be concealed. But when they occur in the king's family, they affect matters of the state, and result in his escape from the son he adores. Will he finds a way to quell the revolt and come back to the City of David?

This is volume III of the trilogy *The David Chronicles*, told candidly by the king himself. David uses modern language, indicating that this is no fairytale. Rather, it is a story that is happening here and now. If you like ancient historical fiction about court intrigue, this king David novel has a modern twist like no book you have read before.

About the Author

U vi Poznansky is a *USA TODAY* bestselling, award-winning author, poet and artist. "I paint with my pen," she says, "and write with my paintbrush."

Uvi earned her B. A. in Architecture and Town Planning from the Technion in Haifa, Israel. During her studies and in the years immediately following her graduation, she practiced with an innovative Architectural firm, taking part in the design of a large-scale project, *Home for the Soldier*.

Having moved to Troy, N.Y. with her husband and two children, Uvi received a Fellowship grant and a Teaching Assistantship from the Architecture department at Rensselaer Polytechnic Institute. There, she guided teams in a variety of design projects and earned her M.A. in Architecture. Then, taking a sharp turn in her education, she earned her M.S. degree in Computer Science from the University of Michigan.

During the years she spent in advancing her career—first as an architect, and later as a software engineer, software team leader, software manager and a software consultant (with an emphasis on user interface for medical instruments devices)— she wrote and painted constantly. In addition, she taught art appreciation classes.

Her versatile body of work can be seen in two websites: her blog includes thoughts about the creative process, reader reviews, author interviews, excerpts from her novels, voice clips from her audiobooks, poems and short stories. Her <u>art site</u> includes bronze and ceramic sculptures, paper engineering projects, oil and watercolor paintings, charcoal, pen and pencil drawings, and mixed media.

Coma Confidential, Overkill, Overdose, and Overdue are novels in the *Ash Suspense Thrillers with a Dash of Romance* series. With each new case, Ash uses grit and intuition to solve the crime.

Virtually Lace is the first volume in a multi-author thriller series, *High-Tech Crime Solvers*, where the authors bring each other's characters into their books.

My Own Voice, The White Piano, The Music of Us, Dancing with Air, and *Marriage before Death* are novels in the *Still Life with Memories* series, a family saga with a love story that develops in the face of hardship and illness over two generations, starting at the 1980's, then harkening back to WWII when Lenny, a soldier, and Natasha, a rising star, first met. These books are also offered in two bundles: *Apart from Love* and *Apart from War*.

Rise to Power, A Peek at Bathsheba, and *The Edge of Revolt* are novels in *The David Chronicles*, telling the story of David as you have never heard it before: from the king himself, telling the unofficial version, the one he never allowed his court scribes to recount. In his mind, history is written to praise the victorious— but at the last stretch of his illustrious life, he feels an irresistible urge to tell the truth. These books are also offered in a trilogy.

In addition, *The David Chronicles* includes six art collections: *Inspired by Art: Fighting Goliath, Inspired by Art: Fall of a Giant, Inspired by Art: Rise to Power, Inspired by Art: A Peek at Bathsheba, Inspired by Art: The Edge of Revolt,* and *Inspired by Art: The Last Concubine.*

A Favorite Son, a new-age twist on an old yarn, is inspired by the biblical story of Jacob and his mother Rebecca, plotting together against the elderly father Isaac, who is lying on his deathbed.

Twisted is a unique collection, laden with shades of mystery. Here, you will come into a dark, strange world, a hyper-reality where nearly everything is firmly rooted in the familiar—except for some quirky detail that twists the yarn.

Home and *Can We Still Love*, Uvi's deeply moving poetry books in tribute of her father, include her poetry and prose as well as translated poems from the pen of her father, the poet, author and artist Zeev Kachel.

Uvi wrote and illustrated two children's books, *Jess and Wiggle* and *Now I Am Paper*. Watch the beautiful animations she created for these books on YouTube.

About the Cover

The cover art for *The Edge of Revolt* is a watercolor painting inspired by a quick charcoal sketch which I have drawn while listening to music--several pieces of music, each with a different rhythm and mood, reflected here.

I imagined that these rhythms are taking me to a magical landscape, which I am yet to explore, and that the edges describe rocks and mountains faraway, and sweeping waves underfoot. Here and there I imagined a figure of a traveler who, like me, is on a journey—but I could not tell if his journey is one of giving chase or one of escape. The more I gaze upon this view, the more detail I find in its edges, which are open to interpretation.

I drew it while in the process of writing about David, reflecting upon the conflicting emotions filling his heart during his escape from his beloved son, Absalom, who has mounted a revolt to topple him from the throne. While the landscape of his journey is that of the mountains of Judea and the Jordan river, the landscape here is abstract, because it reflects the journey you may take, given a great turmoil in your life.

At the top of the title—*The Edge of Revolt*—the letters are bathed in golden light, which fades gradually towards the bottom. Down there, they are soaked in a blood red color, as befits this drama of love, betrayal, and war.

The font style selected for the name of the trilogy—*The David Chronicles*—is a formal, stable one, presented all in capitals. This adheres to the font scheme for the cover of the volume I, *Rise to Power*, and volume II, *A Peek at Bathsheba*.

Together, they are connected both in their art and in the voice of David. I find it amazing to be in his skin from childhood to old age. It has been quite a journey for me, and I hope it would be for you, too.

A Note to the Reader

Thank you for reading this book! I hope you enjoyed it. If you did, I invite you to check out more books from the same pen. There is always a new project on my drawing board, so come back to check it out.

I would love to hear what you thought of this book. You have the power of bringing it to the attention of more readers, by posting your own review. It would mean so much to me.

And another thing you can do to help me spread the word is this: please tell your friends about my work. How else will they hear about the story? How else will the characters, who sprang from my mind onto these pages, leap from there into new minds?

Bonus Excerpts
Excerpt: Rise to Power

To show respect, I fall to my knees before him. The floor is cold, having absorbed the damp of a long winter. The surface is porous, even crumbly here and there, cut of rocks from the Judea mountains. So is the surface of the stage, right in front of my eyes.

I cannot help noting the marks drawn by his spear in the film of dirt up there, around his boots. Scratch, twist, scratch again... No wonder he seems to be in such a royal pain: with all these attendants here to serve him, not a single one has managed to come up with the bright idea of sweeping the floor. They all carry weapons, but not one has a broom.

Sitting nearly immobile, Saul seems as chalky as the walls around him. He sits crumpled—in an odd way—upon the throne. His nails keep digging into the little velvety cushions that are stretched over the carved armrests. Not once does he give a nod in my direction, nor does he acknowledge my presence in any other way.

Which agitates me. It awakens my doubt, doubt in my skill. Much the same as I feel in my father's presence. Repressed. On the verge of acting out.

So, rising to my feet I blurt out, "Your majesty—"

"Don't talk," whispers one of the attendants. "Play."

I am pushed a step or two backwards, so as to maintain proper distance from the presence of the king. My name is called out in a clunky manner of introduction, after which I am instructed to choose from an array of musical instruments. I figure they must be the loot of war. So when I play them, the music of enemy tribes shall resound here, around the hall.

I pluck the strings of a sitar, then put it back down and pick up a lyre, which I make quiver, quiver with notes of fire! Then I rap, clap, tap, snap my fingers, and just to be cute, play a tune on my flute, after which I do a skip, skip, skip and a back flip.

It is a long performance, and towards the end of it I find myself trying to catch my breath. Alas, my time is up. Even so I would not stop.

Entranced I go on to recite several of my poems, which I have never done before, for fear of exposing my most intimate, raw emotions, which is a risky thing for a man, and even riskier for a boy my age. Allowing your vulnerability to show takes one thing above all: a special kind of courage. Trust me, it takes balls.

So, having read the last verse I cast a look at the attendants, especially the ones closest to me. Their faces seem to have softened. I can sense them beginning to adore me. One of them comes over and taps my shoulder, which nearly knocks me off my feet. Another one laughs. Others wipe their eyes.

Then I glance at Saul, hoping for a tear, a smile, a word of encouragement. Instead I note an odd, vacant look on his face.

Utter indifference. It stings me. Am I too short, too young, too curly for the role he has in mind for me?

Wiping the sweat off my brow I bow down before him and turn to leave the court, which is the moment he leans forward on his spear.

"Stop right there," says Saul. "Tell me: what can you do best?"

To which I say, "Recover."

He glowers at me as if to ask, Recover? From what?

"From this," I point out, daring to be honest. "Rejection."

Excerpt: A Peek at Bathsheba

Wrapped in a long, flowing fabric that creates countless folds around her curves, she loosens just the top of it and lets it slide off her head—only to reveal a blush, and mischievous glint, shining in her eye. It is over that sparkle that I catch a sudden reflection, coming from the back window, of a full moon.

Looking left, right, and down the staircase, to make sure no one is lurking outside my chamber door, I let her in. Then I lock it behind her, so no one may intrude upon us.

In a manner of greeting I raise my goblet. It is a gift from my supplier, Hiram king of Tyre, and unlike the other goblets I have in my possession, this one is made of fine glass, with minute air bubbles floating in it. With a big splash I fill it up to the rim with red, aromatic wine. In it I dip a glistening, ruddy cherry, and offer it to her, with a flowery toast.

"For you," I say. "With my everlasting love!"

Bathsheba takes the goblet from my hand, and raises it to her lips. "Love, everlasting?" she says, raising an eyebrow. "What does that mean, in this place?"

I hesitate to ask, "What place is that?"

"This court," she says, with a slight curtsy, "where the signature feature is a harem, which is as big as the king is endowed with glory."

"Glory is a good thing," say I, lowering my voice. "But sometimes it is better to meet in the shadows."

"Especially," she says, matching her voice to mine, "when there are so many others."

"Here we are," say I. "It's just us."

"Really," says Bathsheba, sipping her wine and ever so delightfully, licking her lips. "It must be a special night, then! Just you and me, and no one else, no one else at all."

Yet I cannot avoid feeling the presence of someone other than me in her thoughts, perhaps her husband, Uriah, who is one of my mighty soldiers and the most trusty of them. Earlier today he must have received his transfer orders to join the cavalry in the eastern hills, where he would be stationed outside the city of Rabbah.

I have a catch in my throat as I tell her, "I'm so glad you came."

Bathsheba lifts her eyes and looks straight at me.

"Really," she says, in her most velvety tone. "You mean, I had a choice in this matter?"

Her question stumps me at first, because how can I admit that she is right, so right in asking it? Instead I just shrug.

"You do have a choice," I say at last. "And I hope you'll make it."

"I'm so glad to hear that," says Bathsheba. "With that ape, I mean, that bodyguard of yours knocking so loudly, so rudely, and for such a long time at my door, I had my doubts about it."

"You can go, if you wish," I stress, with a reluctant tone. "But I wish you wouldn't. Stay with me, tonight."

Bathsheba picks the stem of the red cherry, and takes little bites out of it. In her pleasure she hums, and smacks her lips. Then she raises the goblet to my lips, letting me take in the aroma. I do, and then I take a long gulp.

With a slight sway of her hips Bathsheba walks past me, knowing I cannot take my eyes off of her. She wanders about my chamber as if she were the one owning it.

"You've been brought here by my order," I whisper to her, across the space. "But I am the one held captive."

Excerpt: The Music of Us

My son, Ben, has been gone for a month now, staying in some youth hostel in Rome. If I call him, if I stumble into revealing how scared I am that his mother is losing her mind, he may listen. He may heed my fears, grudgingly, and come back here, not even knowing how to offer his support to me. Should I ask for it?

The last thing I wish to do is lean on him for help. He is not strong enough, and whatever the problem may be with her, I can grit my teeth and handle it, somehow, all by myself. Besides, I pray for a spontaneous change in her. I mean, her memory may take a turn for the better just as quickly as it has deteriorated.

Given this hope I decide that for now I will not schedule the head X-Ray that her doctor recommended for her. I figure she has been through so many checkups, so many exams to rule out depression, vitamin B deficiency, and a long list of other possible ailments, all of which has been in vain.

So far, the results have failed to produce a conclusive diagnosis, and this new X-Ray will be no different, because from what I have read, Alzheimer's disease can be determined only through autopsy, by linking clinical measures with an examination of brain tissue. So this new medical hypothesis is just that: a hypothesis. One that cannot be proven; one that cannot go away. An ever-present threat.

Perhaps all she needs is rest. Time, I tell myself. I must give her time. Meanwhile I resolve to keep her condition secret from everyone, especially from my son. Let him enjoy his time away from home, his independence.

Since his departure I called him only once, three weeks ago, and said little, except for blurting out the mundane, "How's Rome?"

"Great," he said vaguely, adding no particulars.

I could not help myself from asking. "So, what about your plans?"

"What about them?"

"D'you have any?"

"For now I have none," he admitted, and immediately changed the subject. "How's mom?"

"Fine."

"Is she?"

"She is," I lied, hoping that the sound of my voice would not betray the tensing of my muscles, the tightening of my jaws.

"Oh good," he said. "Really, really good."

There is only one thing more difficult than talking to Ben, and that is writing to him. Amazingly, having to conceal what his mother is going through makes every word —even on subjects unrelated to her—that much harder. I find myself oppressed by my own self-imposed discipline, the discipline of silence.

And what can I tell him, really? That I keep digging into the past, mining its moments, trying to piece them together this way and that, dusting off each memory of Natasha, of how we were, the highs and lows of the music of us, to find out where the problem may have started?

To him, that may seem like an exercise in futility. For me, it is a necessary process of discovery, one that is as tormenting as it is delightful. If the dissonance in our life would fade away, so will the harmony.

Sometimes I go as far back as the moment we first met, when I was a soldier and she—a star, brilliant yet illusive. Natasha was a riddle to me then, and to this day, with all the changes she has gone through, she still is.

I often wonder: can we ever understand, truly understand each other—soldier and musician, man and woman, one heart and another? Will we ever again dance together to the same beat? Is there a point where we may still touch?

Excerpt: Marriage before Death

Without uttering a sound I gave her a look, begging her to leave. Rochelle gave one to me, begging me to play along.

Out loud she said, "Oh how I hate you! I hate you now more than I ever loved you!"

At that, the SS officer burst out laughing. It lasted quite a while, or so it seemed to me, and by the time it finally ended, a cruel smile was left across his face, stretching from one pointy ear to the other.

"*Ach*," he hissed. "What a woman! Cold one minute—hot the next!"

Rochelle hung her eyes on me one more time.

"At the very least," she implored, "you should say you are sorry, so sorry to have left me in such a difficult situation!"

The SS officer cut in.

"Didn't I tell you?" he asked her. "His kind, they have no morals! Worse than animals is what they are."

She turned away and went back to his side. From there she said, in a tone of regret, "Right you are. I was naive, up to now, to hope for anything different from him."

Over her sorrow, the SS officer went on to say, "How could you ever let yourself be seduced by such a man?"

She shook her head. "How silly of me! How foolish it is to hope! I was sure he would confirm to everyone here his desire to marry me."

To which the SS officer said, "Now, mademoiselle, you have learned your lesson."

She gave him a tearful smile, but then could not help crying out to me, "Oh, for heaven's sake, don't you get it? I'm expecting your child!"

At that I had a change of heart. Why? First, because I was moved to tears by her plea, no matter if it was a fake one or not; and second, because what had I got to lose?

So I uttered, "Forgive me, Rochelle."

"What?" she asked. "What did you say?"

"Forgive me," I said, with a catch in my throat. "If I were a free man I would gladly keep my promise to you."

A triumphant smile played on her red lips. Yet, for just a moment, she was silent.

I thought she might make peace with me, now that I relented. Instead, she turned to the SS officer.

"Herr Müller," she said. "I'm not here to beg for mercy for this man."

In surprise, "You're not?" he asked, raising a thick eyebrow.

And from the other side of the table, his French collaborator echoed, "You're not?"

My face was still burning, still stinging from that slap of hers. I bit my lips to overcome the pain. If I could muster the nerve to speak up once more, I would ask her the very same thing.

Really? You're not?

"No," she stressed.

The toothbrush mustache under Herr Müller's nose started to twitch. Perhaps he was becoming suspicious of her.

"I thought," he said, "that you had a big favor to ask of me."

And she said, "I do."

And he said, "Well? What is it, then?"

"For the sake of my family," said Rochelle, "for the pride of my father, for my own honor, and for the future of this baby, I cannot be an unwed mother! I'd rather die!"

Becoming somewhat impatient, *"Ach!"* he said. "You should have thought of that earlier, before you got involved with the likes of him."

It was then that she said, "I promise, Herr Müller, giving me what I ask for is sure to give you the greatest pleasure, because it is just what this man deserves."

"Which is what?"

"Marriage before death."

Books by Uviart

Coma Confidential

(Volume I of *Ash Suspense Thrillers with a Dash of Romance*)

Kindle: B07L92YHST Paperback: 978-1791691592

Overkill

(Volume II of *Ash Suspense Thrillers with a Dash of Romance*)

Kindle: B084GDK156 Paperback: 979-8644328192

Overdose

(Volume III of *Ash Suspense Thrillers with a Dash of Romance*)

Kindle: B07VP4S6PK Paperback: 978-1086703665

Overdue

(Volume IV of *Ash Suspense Thrillers with a Dash of Romance*)

Kindle: B08S724T4G Paperback: 979-8599499671

Ash Suspense Thrillers: Trilogy

(Volume I-III of *Ash Suspense Thrillers with a Dash of Romance*)

Kindle: B0893MJNSY Paperback: 979-8648269644

Virtually Lace

(Volume I of *High-Tech Crime Solvers*)

Kindle: B07L968RXD Paperback: 978-1790407187

My Own Voice

(Volume I of *Still Life with Memories*)

Kindle: B013TA3FBS Paperback: 978-0984993215

The White Piano

(Volume II of *Still Life with Memories*)

Kindle: B013TAU7L4 Paperback: 978-1517049447

The Music of Us

(Volume III of *Still Life with Memories*)

Kindle: B013TCYWHC Paperback: 978-0-9849932-9-1

Dancing with Air

(Volume IV of Still Life with Memories)

Kindle: B01I4ENROY Paperback: 978-1536896534

Marriage before Death

(Volume V of Still Life with Memories)

Kindle: B0746NW5CD Paperback: 978-1974001736

Apart from Love

(Still Life with Memories Bundle I)

Kindle: B006WPITP0 Paperback: 978-0-9849932-0-8

Apart from War

(Still Life with Memories Bundle II)

Kindle: B07MMZLD7Z Paperback: 978-1792131592

Rise to Power

(Volume I of *The David Chronicles*)

Kindle: B00H6PMZ0U Paperback: 978-0-9849932-4-6

A Peek at Bathsheba

(Volume II of *The David Chronicles*)

Kindle: B00LEPPDV6 Paperback: 978-0-9849932-7-7

The Edge of Revolt

(Volume III of *The David Chronicles*)

Kindle: B00Q5WVKA6 Paperback: 978-0984993284

The David Chronicles: Trilogy

(Volume I-III of *The David Chronicles*)

Kindle: B00QYGF6WG Paperback: 978-1797440699

The David Chronicles: Art

(Volume IV-XI of *The David Chronicles*)

Kindle: B08YWSH7HC Paperback: 979-8721612886

Inspired by Art: Fighting Goliath

(Art book. Volume IV of *The David Chronicles*)

Kindle: B01MSBNSE4   Paperback 978-1797726212

Inspired by Art: Fall of a Giant

(Art book. Volume V of *The David Chronicles*)

Kindle: B01MSBS82Q   Paperback: 978-1092307765

Inspired by Art: Rise to Power

(Art book. Volume VI of *The David Chronicles*)

Kindle: B01N2786VX   Paperback: 978-1092263207

Inspired by Art: A Peek at Bathsheba

(Art book. Volume VII of *The David Chronicles*)

Kindle: B01MUFS9OA   Paperback: 978-1092306225

Inspired by Art: The Edge of Revolt

(Art book. Volume VIII of *The David Chronicles*)

Kindle: B01N6ZG0W8   Paperback: 978-1091306158

Inspired by Art: The Last Concubine

(Art book. Volume IX of *The David Chronicles*)

Kindle: B01N2AXQP2   Paperback: 978-1092302715

A Favorite Son

Kindle: B00AUZ3LGU Paperback: 978-0-9849932-5-3

Twisted

Kindle: B00D7Q3IY4

Paperback: 978-0984993260 Nook: 2940151689588

Home

(Poetry)

Kindle: B00960TE3Y

Paperback: 978-09849932-3-9 Nook: 2940151729468

Can We Still Love

(Poetry)

Kindle: B0GV3G23V4 Paperback: B0GY8Q1Y9Z

Virtually Yummy: Recipes that Inspire

(Cookbook)

Kindle: B085BDNDM5 Nook: 2940163988655

Apple: id1501182051 Kobo: 9781393589853

בית

(Poetry in Hebrew)
Paperback: 978-1494920968

Apple: id1302908918 Kobo: 9781540199966

Jess and Wiggle

Kindle: B013D1W0SM Paperback: 978-1494920968

Now I Am Paper

Kindle: B00YQS4O72 Paperback: 978-1494919429